THAT DAMNED ADAMS & THE AMISTAD

A Novel

Gerald Prueitt

Published by Central Park South Publishing 2024
www.centralparksouthpublishing.com

This novel is based on events from 1800 to 1841 from public domain articles, letters, notes, and from Library Of Congress research. While many events, locations, and people are based on historical facts—the author has used imagination and dialogue to draw disparate events together to be as close as possible to characters and events of the time, in his opinion.

Typesetting and e-book formatting services by Victor Marcos

ISBN:
978-1-956452-61-7 (pbk)
978-1-956452-62-4 (hbk)
978-1-956452-63-1 (ebk)

"WHAT IS PAST IS PROLOGUE."

—William Shakespeare, The Tempest.

May 17th, 1838

A raucous, drunk, cursing, torch-carrying, anti-abolition mob swarmed past the abolitionist editor WL Garrison—fortunately unrecognized. Much threatened, he had an anti-abolitionist five-thousand-dollar price on his head. The vastly outnumbered police decided retreat was the most logical part of valor as fifteen thousand pro-slavers stormed the Pennsylvania Hall and set it on fire.

Also caught up in the flood tide of zealots, and new to Philadelphia, was abolitionist John Greenleaf Whittier. Too new in town to be recognized, he charged in with the mob and managed to bag some of the papers and books from his just finished office before the inferno took the building. His poem "Don't Quit" may not have come to him in this moment, but it was forming. Being a Quaker poet, his tract was a bit less incendiary than the mob's as he wrote that week, in flowery prose, of the just completed building: "We dedicate our fair and lofty hall, pillar and arch, entablature and wall, as virtue's shrine, as Liberty's abode, sacred to Freedom and the Freedom's God."

Whittier had just arrived in Philadelphia and set up the offices of The Pennsylvania Freeman in the newest, most modern, and largest building in Pennsylvania. Shocked by the violence of the mob, the Quaker Whittier managed to stuff much of his work in a croker sack and save it. The next day he wrote:

"ATROCIOUS OUTRAGE! BURNING
OF PENNSYLVANIA HALL!—Eighteenth
day of the fifth month 1838.

Half past seven o'clock—Pennsylvania Hall is in ashes!

The beautiful temple consecrated to Liberty has been offered as a smoking sacrifice to the demon of slavery." The Anti-Slavery Convention of American Women met in the street in front of the still smoldering ashes the next morning to elect officers.

And what was that burning expression of freedom all about? Taking away the freedom to own slaves. Some Americans didn't want to know or care about the slavery problem. Others were violently pro-slavery, their fortunes depending on slavery to expand into the new Western frontier. Then there were those other radical agitators, the abolitionists, who were also set to explode.

Anger vibrated the air, amplifying the bedlam clatter of horse hooves, street venders hawking, and the metal bindings of wagon wheels grinding over cobbles on the busy city streets. But that fracas was tranquil compared to the so called "United" States Congress in session. Their lawn may have once been a tranquil cow pasture, and a gentle wind did keep most blood sucking mosquitoes down in the swamp, but up on the hill a bloody eruption was building.

The sun streamed into the congressional chamber, past the stars and stripes wafting in the light breeze of open windows. It was an elegant room by the day's standards. A lot of hand tooling in the furnishings and woodwork of stars, eagles, and bunting is meant to add stature to the men who make up the United States government.

While its's true John Quincy Adams had a pet alligator in the East Wing bathroom, when he was president, it was nowhere as wild as the daily battles 1.2 miles down the street. Adams was always the biting voice raised above the confused noise of that contumacious chamber called Congress whenever they debated slavery.

John Quincy Adams thrived at returning outright insults to pro-slavers in the senate. In returning a slur to an Alabama speaker who denigrated African women, he once said, "If they are infamous women, who was it that made them infamous? Not their own color—but their masters." Adams pivoted slightly as he addressed the mob of the House—unperturbed as a spittoon sailed by, splashed past representative Clay, and bounced off the next desk. Clay bounded across the aisle to stop two attackers heading to John Quincy. Above the growing roar, Adams chortled in his most trenchant tone and continued, "In the South there exists a great resemblance between the progeny of the colored people and the white men who claim possession of them. Thus, perhaps, the charge of infamous might be retorted on those who made it as originating from themselves."

An Alabama representative took three running leaps and vaulted onto the top of the New York representative's desk, bounded across four more desks, aiming for Adams but swinging his cane at Clay, who stopped it with his own in front of John Quincy. Clay, who often argued with Adams, ducked and landed a hard right hook into the Alabamian's privates. Several dozen irate gentlemen surged into the fray as the speaker broke his gavel pounding for order while a dozen representatives struggled in the aisle, fell over three quarreling hounds and bashed each other with anything handy.

Three of the jumble rammed into John Quincy Adam's aide, James. Two other young pages shoved back. One leapt into the mob and slipped on a chicken leg and a clutter of papers strewn across the floor. The quarrel kicked over eight spittoons and fell onto the pack of dogs still fighting over the chicken. Calhoun, once a friend of Adams, and a dozen men joined in. The fight nearly cleared the room as they pushed to the outer corridor.

Southerner Benton smiled contemptuously and winked at Adams. Across the aisle, and behind a wall of battling representatives, Hayes was heard shouting over the fracas, "Our slaves are our machinery, and we have as good a right to profit by them as do the northern men who profit by the machinery they employ."

Thomas Hart Benton, senator from Missouri, shoved Sen. Henry Foote for insulting him, Foote pulled a pistol, but four others in the scuffle separated them without incident. He was heard explaining, "There was a clear shot. I wouldn't have hit anyone else."

Some Congressmen managed, amazingly, to sleep during this brouhaha, some ate, and the rest yelled or charged at the opposition. Congress was a pigpen. Benton, chewing on a half a chicken watched John Quincy Adams darkly, then heaved the carcass in Adams's direction, missed, cursed, wiped his hands on his vest, and nodded at the two men who delivered some papers to him. Stevenson, Polk, Bell, Calhoun, Southard, and Wilde, all gathered in a cluster shouting at each other.

Adams turned and imperiously referred to the Constitutional clause that counted each slave as three-fifths of a free person that calculated how many congressmen each state would have. "Now those so-called machines have twenty-odd Representatives in this Hall, Representatives elected not by their machines, but by those who own them…Have the Northern manufacturers asked for representation for their machines? Their looms and factories have no vote in Congress…Everybody knows that where this type of Southern machinery exists there is liable to be more violence than elsewhere because their machinery sometimes exerts self-moving power." Two dozen men clashed on the floor as the fight pushed into the corridor. One Kentuckian charged into the brawl, drew his pistol, and shot a guard in the leg.

We interrupt this fight to bring you a little background.

A little background: It was a time when the infinite pieces of the American puzzle looked like they would never fit together. It was a time when leaders of nations gobbled up or got gobbled up by other lands around the globe. Parts of Africa, India, South America, and North America were waiting to be taken by France, England,

Spain, the Netherlands, and Portugal, who bled their colonial empires. After the American revolution settled down, a new century started and opened the dirtiest time in American politics. The early 1800s were full of privately owned printing presses and anyone with a complaint ran off hundreds of handbills, or "newspapers" to spread their surrogate truth—whether it was true or not.

It was not yet the worst of times—but they were building. The 1800s were a time of slander, lies, greed, defamation, and hyperbole; some just called the whole mess 'political plater,' a word also used for a low-grade horse. But harsh talk and violent threats left little room for diplomacy in America those days. Plater was the rarely truthful, made-up, spurious style of congressional debate that peaked during Andrew Jackson's administration causing a lot of Americans to curse both houses of government, both major parties, and the horses they rode in on.

No lie was too outrageous; during the rough and tumble campaign muckrakers from both sides attacked both Jackson and Adams. Andrew Jackson's wife, Rachel, was traumatized by the personal attacks on her second marriage accusing her of being a bigamist, had chest pains, became ill, and died on December 22, 1828. Jackson accused the Adams campaign, and Henry Clay of causing her death, saying, "I can and do forgive all my enemies. But those vile wretches who have slandered her must look to God for mercy." Politics were going to get even meaner.

Abolitionist Adams was a thorn in the side of the South. He had put hundreds of petitions against the atrocity of slavery and for the fair treatment of Native Americans before a hostile congress. The great majority of these were tabled. This Meant the petitions were not heard and were not brought forward to be voted on, because the Jacksonians outnumbered the abolitionists and controlled the House. This was just one of the reasons Congress was so contentious.

There were so many reasons so many plots were boiling in the states, and so many of them did not seem to have anything to do with each other, but they were all happening because of the politics of a cabal of the same men.

A major cause: Before 1821, before the Aztecs, before the Tlaxcallan, before 300 years of Spanish rule, vast stretches of land Spain called 'the Viceroyalty of New Spain' stretched from Baja California to Canada, to the Southwest, and all of Central America, except Panama were ceded to Mexico from Spain. This huge territory was the pre-history home to Pueblos, Navaho, Comanche, Apaches, Hopis, Kiowa, Tenewa, and Yamparika, the native peoples in the north who had fought Spanish, Mexican, and European ambitions to claim their land for centuries. Mexicans called them *bárbaros*.

At the end of 300 years of colonization Spain left to Mexico what was a huge land mass, covering almost everything from what is now Washington state to Brazil. Mexico quickly claimed the entire region to stop colonization and exploitation by Europe and America. But it was way too large for the new Mexico to hold. By 1855 Mexico was less than half the country it had been at its foundation in 1821. Central America cut itself from Mexico in 1823, and few wanted to argue with Simón Bolivar "El Libertador" the revolutionary who led the establishment of Venezuela, Bolivia, Colombia, Ecuador, Peru, and Panama.

However, at the same time avaricious pro-slaver investors, industrialists, shipping magnates from Boston to Atlanta, and their bought congressmen all coveted the new land called Mexico, the rationale being that Southern States could create a vast new slavery state in the new territory and abolitionists couldn't do anything about it.

There were some strange bedfellows in the politics of the time that caused later vendettas: Calhoun ran as vice president for both antagonists Adams and Jackson. But contrarian Adams won with a parliamentary ploy by Clay. In those days the candidate who got the most votes, that equaled a majority, were elected president. The next candidate with the second-most votes was elected vice president, no matter what party they belonged to. When no one won a majority of the electors, or when several contestants tied, the house would hold an election for the presidency. Jackson won the popular vote with 152,901 and had 99 electoral votes to Adams's 114,023 popular with 84 electoral votes, 32 fewer than he needed for a majority and thus the presidency.; Clay won 47,217, and Crawford 46,979. Crawford had 41 votes for third place—and there were 37 for Clay who was fourth and thus not counted, but with his behind-the-scenes maneuvering he was able to swing enough of his electoral states to give Adams the win. Jackson claimed the election was rigged and that he had won both the popular vote and the electoral vote, and that the presidency had been stolen from him by the double-dealing Clay.

Adams was an abolitionist Yankee and proud of it, while Jackson believed exclusive privileges like aristocracy and monopolies were poison to the common man and that the majority should rule, and the rights of the community overruled the individual—strange beliefs for a man who owned over a hundred slaves. He thought that was just the natural order of things. He seemed to have justified to himself that they were prisoners taken by other Africans, sold to Europeans, and shipped to the Americas—not unlike the British who sent their prisoners as labor shipping them as indentured servants to Australia and America. Well, except they were set free after their time of servitude.

Congress wrote the tariff act of 1828 to protect the industrial North when John Quincy Adams was president. It was passed on May 19th during the presidency of Andrew Jackson. It was labeled "The Tariff of Abominations" by the Southern block because it protected the Northern industrial states from cheaper European goods. But many in the South felt they had to pay much higher prices for imports from Europe. So, they argued, that made it difficult for the European market to buy Southern cotton, the major export of the south. It would be a festering sore point for the next twenty years. Polk was advisor for Jackson's smear campaign and victory over Adams when Jackson ran for president in 1828. Polk became one of the new President's most loyal supporters in the House.

Adams was a Whig and the most vocal agitator in the pro-slaver Congress. One of his few printable nicknames was "old man eloquent." He had a long history in politics, so few were surprised when ran for Congress, won, and became the scourge of the Jackson administration. Adams had, after all, arranged the United States purchase of Florida from Spain, the Transcontinental Treaty, which established the border between Spanish and American land holdings, all during the Monroe administration.

Joshua Giddings, representative of Ohio was a foul-mouthed opponent of slavery. Known for egalitarian racial actions and nearly self-educated, he passed the Ohio bar exam in 1821 and spent sixteen years as an attorney and abolitionist ally of Adams.

Giddings refused to be intimidated by Jackson and Polk's increasingly ambitious arguments for war. His diatribes became so annoying that a Virginian newspaper offered $10,000 for his capture alive or $5,000 dead. In 1846 Congressman Giddings argued that the then president Polk's aggressive maneuvers were designed to provoke a war with Mexico and that Jackson and Polk's ultimate goal was always the conquest of Mexico and California. So, when Mexico won its independence from Spain in 1821, American and European raiders, homesteaders, and adventurers followed thousands of wagons into Texas California, Oregon, and Washington. It was hardly a secret land rush; the idea was to usurp the region from Mexico. So, there were boatloads of Europeans, by the tens of thousands. Many who could barely speak English.

Every European country was having its bourgeois revolution but especially Ireland, France, Italy, Germany, and Poland. Ireland alone had sent over two hundred and fifty thousand Gaelic speaking famine-destroyed farmers to the new world. Potato, wheat, and corn crops were a disaster in Europe in the 1830s and 40s. This European flood of new immigrants furthered American territorial ambitions enraging Mexico.

Giddings shouted over the eternal ruckus that was congress, "In the murder of Mexicans upon their own soil, or in robbing them of their country, I can take no part, either now or hereafter. The guilt of these crimes must rest on others; I will not participate in them; but if Mexicans or any other people should dare invade our country, I would meet them with the sword in one hand and a torch in the other. We may always justify ourselves for defending our country, but never for waging a war upon an unoffending people for the purpose of conquest."

Calhoun laughed at Giddings and said, "Hell, the Mex's ain't been a country longer'n my baby boy. An, got no more sense."

The United States was growing. There was the Anti-Masonic Party, an energetic, third, single issue party, that grabbed a dozen seats solely on the distrust of freemasonry. Even though presidents George Washington, James Monroe, Andrew Jackson, James K. Polk, and James Buchanan, were freemasons. The Whig party were nationalists, and for internal improvements and westward expansion. The Democrats touted states' rights and less government, anti-federal bank, pro-agriculture, and less big industry. They believed in westward expansion. The Democratic Republican party, which grew out of the Republican party's attitude was: there are no boundaries, no end to the riches of the land; it's all there for the taking, regardless of what or who went before. And briefly the OSSB—Order of the Star Spangled Banner, or the Know Nothing Party, a white Protestant, anti-Catholic secret society. Thus the cast, plot, and stage was set for some event to cause what would became Civil War. It was a time where innocence was lost. A time as full of blackguards, libertine slavers, brigands, pirates, freebooters, intrigue, twists, turns, racism, and almost as much violence as a Tarentino movie—and it foretold the coming war between the states.

CHAPTER ONE

June 30th, 1839

The name on its bow was the *Amistad*. The ship's battered letters in Spanish means 'Friendship'. A slave ship out of Havana, the *Amistad* was barely seen through the night sea spray. Unheard in the shrill voice of the building storm it's weathered wooden eagle figurehead soared through the building spray of whitecaps. The hurricane roared around the ship and down the below deck grating, bellowing like the voice of Ngewo, the Mende sky god and supreme power who created the universe. Lightning flashed. The ship's eagle figurehead surged out of the white foam of a storm wave that roared over the gunnels and flooded the deck. Flash! The word *"AMISTAD"* shined through foam and rain—then disappeared, swallowed under another large wave.

Capt. Ramon Ferrer had long experience of beating the odds and out foxing British cruisers off the coast of Cuba. Through a network of Cuban lookouts, slavers knew exactly where the British ships hunted and warned the slave ships. The captain of the Amistad knew the coastal harbors, inlets, coves, and currents of the 3,500-mile Cuban coast. That made the Royal Navies search for slave ships very difficult.

It was a dark night, with a brooding overcast sky and a stiff wind. The Amistad was running without lights, following the coast off Isabela de Sagua. It had been a long day for Captain Ferrer. In the morning he and a crew of six oversaw the loading of his ship with cargo, both human and non-human, at the bustling Havana docks. There was a biblical sunset with dramatic Caribbean colors of light streaming through the building clouds. He had been at the ship's wheel for six hours when the weather shifted dramatically.

Beneath the deck, darker than the night storm, a black man scratched at black pig-iron slave collar. Black bodies laid out head to head, foot to foot. Black men in a pitch-black hole. Cinque the slave, once Cinque the free man, worked a black iron stub of nail, and scratched at a lock, poking it, twisting, prying for freedom. Then a sound. Click. Irons fell to floor. The chain was free.

Black shapes moved slowly in the darkness. Unwinding bodies crawled over one another, stiff with weeks of being chained in cramped quarters. Slowly Cinque pulled the heavy chain through his black iron collar and handed it to the next slave, who looked up wide eyed in surprise, then the chain moved to the next and the next.

No words were said, no words were needed, and could not be heard anyhow in the deafening drum like beat of waves that sounded as the bow rose and fell, hitting the waves. *Boom, boom, boom.* Shifting cargo rolled in the hold adding to the jarring motion of the ship at storm. Cinque stretched, and cat-like moved toward the stairwell. He paused, taking one small lantern to light another lamp that cast flickering orange light over his bloody wrists. The lamps swung crazily with the sea surge causing light to circle and swim in angry shifting shadows changing the shapes of enslaved men into demons that seemed to break apart and float forward like angry apparitions from the darkness, then reform out of the shifting gloom. There was so much storm noise that Cinque wasn't worried anyone would hear him release the chain that rattled through the iron grating, but he didn't know how many were on deck.

Cautiously, Cinque moved to the stairwell leading from the cargo hold. Three silhouettes followed. Lightning flashes glared through the iron bars overhead. Fearful shadows stopped as a barrel crashed past them and slammed into a post and spilt open. Eyes used to the darkness watched a crate full of crockery collide with another barrel of silks and scatter their contents. They pulled apart a dozen stacked crates as barrels and smaller crates were broken open. One crate, full of cane knives scattered out ominously sharp black iron blades. The timorous shadows grabbed at the machetes, stood, and spoke quickly in Mende but no words were needed—they were armed.

The Africans, finally able to stand, stretched in the Amistad stairwell, deeply inhaling the fresh storm air charging down on them. Others crawled from dark chambers that were only three feet ten inches from floor to ceiling, the stairwell was the only place they could stand upright. More joined the group; Tomba laughed at the flash of lightning glaring off the blade he hefted. Cinque quieted him with an angry look. Laughter is unheard on a slave ship. They spoke with gestures and quietly formed a plan. They edged upward into the salt spray of the grating and the storm-raked deck.

A maelstrom of saint Elmo's fire danced off masts and booms like lingering charges of lightning. Rain and sea spray washed over the deck and rigging, as the Amistad entered the storm's eye-wall. Winds that spiraled over the ship caused the painful sound of the wood hull fighting against the storm. The sounds of the ship's tossing, twisting, and pulling from stem to stern was almost as loud as the thunder of the storm.

Cinque covered his eyes against the salt spray, and four others fell back into the hold. Which was worse—the Hell above or Hell below? Cinque shook the water out of his eyes, slid the heavy grating back, and smiled at the rush of fresh air and the cold spray of salt sea and rain. He handed the lamp down to Garbo and raised his head and shoulders to deck level and looked around quickly; an iridescent glow disappeared into the clouds; flashes of lightning showed no one on deck except the pilot at the stern fighting the weather at the giant helm.

Cinque stepped up a rung on the stairs and lifted himself topside. He reached for a lanyard, stretched, and inhaled deeply, cleaning his lungs of foul below decks air. Others slipped out quickly, holding on to each other they scanned the heaving deck. The helmsman fought as much to stand against the waves and wind as to keep the ship right. Slipping through the shadows, one by one, fifteen figures disappeared fore and aft into the storm's darkness.

Cinque, nearly unseen in the downpour, drenched in sea water, ducked around the mast and moved quickly to the portal to the captain's cabin. He pushed the door open and slowly stepped inside. Lightning outlined Cinque in the doorway as he cautiously moved forward. Treading awkwardly in the hallway, balancing a tray, the black cook bumped along the wall as he battled the storm, trying to steady the captain's coffee.

In the captain's cabin, exhausted from hours at the helm wrestling with the squall, the captain fell fully dressed on his bunk and rolled with the pitch of the ship. Cinque closed the door but the room still sounded like the storm. Cinque lifted his blade slowly—the ship's cook screamed from the interior doorway. The captain sat up wide eyed, swung his feet across the bunk and dodged as— *slash*! Cinque's blade missed. The captain rolled, grabbed his saber handle, tossed the scabbard, and ran around the table. Shocked awake, the storm noise, the shifting room, and the panicked cook added to the captain's confusion.

The captain pushed through the portal to the deck and shoved the cook into Cinque who rushed forward as the captain slammed the portal. The cook was gutted from the savage sweep of Cinque's blade. Waves overran the deck knocking the captain off his feet.

Two of the slaves on deck charged at the captain but were no match for a fencer of his expertise. The captain shouted an alarm to all hands and dodged around the main mast. Cinque kicked the cabin door open and was hit with a broadside wave that washed him across the deck and into a bilge pump handle, he grabbed it and struggled up looking for the captain. Four Africans rushed the captain swinging their machetes. He held them at bay, ducking behind storm-loosened rigging, grabbed a line with a heavy triple dead eye and swung it at the first African around the mast and slammed him in the head. Slipping behind a yardarm he slashed at the three men several times, but bloodied they kept coming.

Pelted with rain, blinded with seawater, the captain franticly twisted his blade free of one attacker as Cinque ran at him and swung a machete slashing the captain's head open. The captain bounced against the rail blood spurting out of him as he fell overboard.

Montez gasped as the captain disappeared in the twenty-foot wave that then washed him back on board and across the deck. Ruiz grabbed Montez and they were chased across the deck into the hold. There, in total darkness, they crashed into walls and cargo, then managed to squeeze into the shallow storage bins. Montez dived under some canvas behind stacked barrels.

A dozen Africans, shouting back and forth in three different African dialects, searched the shifting storage area with torches. Some were distracted by a barrel of salt pork that had crashed and scattered. Others found Montez and Ruiz, pulled them from hiding, and dragged them on deck where Cinque stopped the slaves from killing the two Spaniards.

More slaves poured out of the hold onto a deck that was a bloody battleground with screams of anger, panic, and pain. Lightning flashed as slaves ran the length of the ship. Three of the crew struggled to untie a lifeboat. Forty slaves rushed on deck yelling to build their courage against the crew and storm.

With no one at the helm, the ship rolled, nearly broaching, and sent all on deck sprawling. The Africans were pushed to the bow by a sea surge but managed to scramble up and corner three of the crew who dodged and tried to fight but were hacked to death. Two crew members managed to release a lifeboat from the stern and disappeared into the sounding gale.

Dark silhouettes in a dark night closed in on the three remaining survivors. Cinque stepped in front of them and held up his blade. Cinque saved the only three survivors: Ruiz, Antonio, and Montez. He shouted angrily at the slaves that the three could be used as bartering in case some evil wind of fate sent the Spanish ships. Ruiz pointed at the free spinning wheel and desperately tried to tell them that the rolling of the ship would sink it if no one steered.

Blood let and tensions purged, the slaves rummaged through the hold and found rum. Drunk on rum and freedom, they scoured the ship's hold, scattering crockery, olives, rice, and bolts of material over the decks. Cinque never left the three captives and simply watched the other Africans plunder the ship, releasing months of degradation from Africa to Cuba, having lived cramped and naked in slave pens like cattle in that fetid hold. As the storm quieted, the ship went slack sailed. Some of the Africans wore the crew's clothing, while others were naked to the soft sea air, and some draped themselves in fine Spanish table linen. Some Africans slept on deck, and some were sick, having gorged themselves on barrels of olives and pickled meat.

Quiet. A small ship lost against the vast ocean. The eagle figurehead on the bow caught the morning sun. The two Spanish captives were chained to the mast in slave collars. Cinque sat cross legged watching the sun rise. He knew that was east. He remembered the few times he and his chain line were allowed on deck of the ship from Africa. He remembered the lay of the mast shadows and the direction of the sun while on deck. Cinque then moved among the slaves for the first time, arousing, challenging, giving orders in Mende. He clanged the captain's blade against the chain of the Spaniard and cabin-boy Antonio and pointed to the sun. In simple but clear language he said, "Return to Africa."

Then Cinque spoke to Antonio in Mende , Cinque's language. Pointing to the sun and following eastward with his gaze. Antonio had difficulty understanding Cinque's dialect. Then he had to translate it into Spanish, which was slightly different from the Cuban language he picked up at the slave auction pens. He was frightened and very cautious about what he said, slowly repeating each word and pronouncing both Mende and Spanish with great caution. The Spaniards looked on, waiting for the translation. The other slaves, frustrated at Antonio's slow progress, joined in, pushing forward angrily. Each shouted their own demands and clarifications. Cinque ordered them back, shouted for quiet. He held the sword to Antonio's face and almost whispered, "Tell them take us back to Mende land."

The translation was crude. Nurnah, a slave, spoke Congolese to Antonio. Antonio, born in the Congo, had a slight knowledge of Mende. Antonio translated into Spanish for Ruiz and Montez who had both owned slaves from Lango and Angola whose language was not even close to a language Cinque knew. They were all Africans and this should seem simple — but Africa had almost two thousand languages.

Finally, with sign language and the near translation of Antonio, Montez could hardly believe his ears. He gasped and shook his head. Using his hands, desperately trying to signal the impossibility of what Cinque asked, Montez looked to Antonio and in Spanish and English he struggled to make the Africans understand. He motioned to Ruiz for support. "Return to Africa?! No! You can't be serious. Wait. Tell him it is impossible! This ship is not made for that kind of voyage. Too far. Too much water. And, my God, no food. Bad sun. Need fresh water. And there is no crew!"

"Return to Africa." Cinque repeated coldly.

CHAPTER TWO

July 2nd, 1839

Cinque motioned for the sails to be hoisted. The Africans pulled at the ropes that sprawled all over the storm-riddled deck. Canvas unfurled and the wind caught the mast swung out banging against the rails. The African "crew" jumped away and held their ears. Cinque shouted at them and they all stood aside. He quickly turned to Ruiz and Montez, pointed the captain's blade at Montez, and then to the sail. It was a slow process but with the cabin boy almost understanding, Montez was able to show the Africans how to work the sails and rigging. It was complicated and tedious, but they learned quickly. Cinque watched everything Montez did. Antonio was prodded by Cinque and in no uncertain terms told to help Montez get the ship ready to sail. Watching the sword point wave around the ship Antonio quickly told Montez and Ruiz what Cinque wanted. With the compass and sextant charms strung around his neck and the captain's sword and scabbard roped around his waist—the symbols of power—no-one questioned Cinque's leadership, no-one questioned his directions.

After spending the morning walking a dozen Africans through the workings of the rigging and sails Cinque followed Montez through the ship as Montez checked the water, compass, sextant, and rigging. They entered the captain's quarters and Montez reached for the captain's desk. Cinque froze Montez with a quick sword blade to his neck. He knocked Montez and Ruiz against the wall. Cinque rummaged through the captain's desk tossing books and clothes to the floor. He slammed the top-drawer lock with a quick blade thrust. The drawer dropped open and Cinque grabbed two pistols. Cinque laughed and returned his sword to its scabbard. He cocked a flintlock and waved it at the two Spaniards. Montez pointed at a map rack and laid the top map on the table, he pointed at himself then Cinque and waved at the ship around them, put his finger on the map, and ran it from Cuba to where he thought they were now. Nervously he pored over the captain's log and charts, memorizing directions, distances, islands, and the closest American coastal towns.

On the days the slaves had been herded up on deck in shackles, the hunter Cinque had tracked the sun across the sky, marking the trail of the big slave ship from Africa. Now he motioned to Montez to hoist sail; they would return. Cinque knew their destination must be toward the sun; twice he had seen the captain sighting them with his magic instruments, but he didn't know the incantations, chants, or secrets. So, he hung the magic around his neck and had to leave the night sailing to the Spaniard. Montez was less frightened now; he knew that he was needed to sail them to safety.

They told Antonio to explain to the Africans: "First they would have to re-supply their food and water." Montez said he had spotted four small islands, the Turks and Caicos and the chain to the Bahamas that could help them. It took a lot of explaining that—Yes, the sun is over there, and Africa is way over there—but there are no islands between here and Africa and they cannot sail for three weeks without food and water. Cinque glared at the two, punched Antonio in the chest with each word, and growled. "No food and water on island? You all will die. Then we will go to Africa."

In two days a small island was sighted. Two Africans hanging in the rigging shouted excitedly in Mende. Half an hour later, with an inexperienced crew, the Amistad sailed two hundred yards from shore—too close.

Montez shouted at Cinque and Kimbo the helmsman, "Fast starboard, down the sails. Down the sails! Shallow water. See." The "crew" all looked at Montez blankly. He stared over the rail at the too-shallow water getting even more shallow fast.

Ruiz shouted, "Come about! Come about! Take the sails down. Down!"

It's called 'beam reach' and this was a bad time for it. The cross wind hit the sails. Half a dozen Africans Montez had schooled in two-hour lessons of managing the sails, rushed to lines, pulled battens, and did anything they thought they remembered and several things they didn't. *Bang!* echoed around the little harbor as the mainsail boom swung around and knocked over a dozen Africans. Three scampered up the rigging and—*Bang!* The tattered foresail dropped. Four Africans ended up in the bay, strangely, their ignorance saved them from heeling everything on deck overboard.

An exasperated Montez ducked under a snapped baggywrinkle line, shook his head and said, "Drop the anchor. Loose the yawl boat."

A group from the Amistad rowed ashore carrying empty barrels. Any break from the ship was a welcome change, and best of all they were going to be on mother earth. So they rowed in unison singing Mende country songs. The fear of sinking behind them, the sun shone, the wind was low and behind the rise of the island. The group splashed into clear water and onto the beach. Two of the group ran across white sand, scaled the sandy ledge, past a stand of red mangrove, and into the low shrub. They stopped at the top of the first rise and scanned the thick vegetation.

On the far North of the island lay a mysterious, deep blue hole that was salt water. Antonio shook his head and said "Old sailors tell the story of the Lusca that live in those holes, giant octopuses bigger than our ship. Not safe." They all went "Ahhh," and hacked their way inland with their machetes. As the tangle got thicker they reached a knoll of an overlook. A sea of pink Flamingos, thousands of flamingos, feeding on fish and crabs, then there were turtles, ducks, egrets and their eggs in nests among the mangroves. The African assault plan on the nests was like an army confrontation.

Half of the group went on looking for water. Fuliwulu stopped dramatically and laughed. Ba and Sessi looked at him like he'd finally lost it. Fuliwulu pointed at a stand of trees with clusters of bright yellow fruit. He climbed the first of the trees and started throwing papayas at his band. Foraging wild fruit and stuffing themselves as they went the happy group bantered back and forth. Then—*Bang, bang, bang*. Shots. They all ducked at once and waited. Two more shots in the distance. Fakina signaled for two of the group of six to cautiously climb one of the vine-covered trees and scout the area. Kale hand signaled, "A group of half a dozen whites and as many natives hunt boar."

The forager group ran to the water group, motioning for them to be quiet. The entire troop climbed a small hilltop and watched the white hunters shoot three boars. All the white men carried long rifles and pistols. The Amistad Africans quietly hurried back to the beach, pulled their skiff from the bushes, and rowed back to the ship.

That evening Cinque gave the ship over to Montez, who continued to sail in the direction of Africa with Cinque watching closely—until the sun was down and the horizon was totally dark. Then slowly Montez turned the wheel, watching the sail; then as a breeze stiffened, he turned harder and harder. He stood at the wheel all night watching the stars. As the night lightened and before the sun morphed into a misshapen egg shape on the horizon, Montez slowly came about and pointed the bow East. The next day the same routine: sail to the sun by day, by night Montez tacked towards the Americas.

The second storm hit at dawn. With a crack crew, sailing the Amistad in open water was difficult at best. But with the shallow draft ship, and a crew of seasick natives…it was a near disaster. Only Cinque, Nurnah and Antonio with Montez worked through the storm; the rest were helplessly sick.

On June 12th, 1839, the storm moved on. Montez, Ruiz, Antonio and Cinque walked the deck and took toll of the storm: more shredded sails, lines fouled, and one broken mast. Ruiz kicked the side of one their four polluted water barrels, growling "Jesucristo, the damn water's fouled." Montez unfurled a map. "Tell him we must stop again for water. We have to find land—West is land. West to get water."

Antonio, eyes huge, turned to Cinque and pointed West. "Water. Yes, new water. There—water—land."

Cinque pointed East, "Back to Africa."

"Africa?" Ruiz laughed in disbelief.

Montez glared at Ruiz, "Yes, yes, Cinque I understand. But it is too far that way. First," he points West, "go for water, then Africa. Remember how long you were on the big ship from Africa to Cuba? This smaller ship will take longer—not so many sails. Right?"

Ruiz added, "That's bad, we will all die without water." Cinque shook his head, exhausted, he ordered the two Spaniards chained to the mast, entered the captain's cabin, and collapsed on the bunk.

Chained to the mast, Ruiz sighed, closed his eyes and remembered leaving Spain as a young man. His family were serfs, struggling just to feed themselves after the 1812 revolution—the king was kicked out. Then barely ten years later Ruiz watched helplessly as the army of the "hundred thousand sons of Saint Louis"—that was the French army—came to save the Spanish royalists and restore King Ferdinand to absolute power. Ruiz's taste of freedom led him out into the world, and this is how he was to end up? A slave, or worse, murdered by slaves.

Exhausted, he fell asleep. At sunrise the slaves roamed the deck, frightened, thirsty, and weary, three tried to drink salt water. Ruiz stopped them.

"No. No. Antonio tell them that if they drink the ocean water they will die. Too much salt." Antonio looked back and forth at the ocean and, Gnakwoi, Kwong, and Pungwune leaning over the railing with a bucket. He shrugged and said, "They don't believe."

Ruiz rattled his chains and shouted. "I don't drink it. I'm thirsty too!"

Nervously looking at the captain's cabin door, where Cinque was sleeping, a dozen Africans led by Kwong crowded around Antonio, spoke low and fast in a jumble of languages. They asked Antonio to ask Montez and Ruiz to take them back.

"They want go back to island. There are crabs and bird eggs and there is fruit and water. They saw black men in the hunting for pig. They safe on land."

Ruiz turned to Montez, they glanced at the captain's cabin where Cinque was sleeping. "Are they revolting against Cinque?"

The three-way translation started again. Montez spoke to Antonio quickly and quietly. "Tell them there is safety on land—water, food." Montez smiles, adding, "And black women!"

The Africans huddled, all nodding in agreement. Kwong stepped from the group and pointed to where Montez had pointed. "Pra va dance, yes?"

Montez and Ruiz sat course for New Providence.

With the wind at their backs Ruiz smiled, "Ah, amigo, the veil of darkness has been lifted."

Looking at the happy group watching from the bow, Montez sighed, "Not so loud my friend. Not so loud."

The Africans danced, swayed, a few chanted love songs.

A cool breeze wafted over Cinque, the sound of his wife singing outside his compound as the tribe thrashed rice on a mat, and then shook the straw mat letting the wind take away the hulls. He smiled and turned on his side. Cinque opened his eyes. He sat up, realized he was not at home in his Mende village. Why sing? They are not home. Startled by the singing he jumped out of bed and ran on deck. He looked at the sun, struck Ruiz unconscious, and angrily grabbed the helm.

Shouting a torrent of Mende from the wheel, Cinque cowered the slaves. Kwong frowned at them, stepped forward and pounded his chest. "We need food and water. You are not my king. I say we need to stop and see this land."

Cinque unfurled the captain's whip, which he wore as a symbol of authority. Cinque grabbed Antonio and shoved him in front of the wheel, unfurling the whip; he snapped it and shouted at the group to hold Kwong over a barrel.

Kwong resisted, twisting he shouted, "You will all die to follow blind."

"We must follow the sun. Return to Africa. Hold him. There is law here. This is law," Cinque said, and struck Kwong again and again.

Mendez watched, wincing with every lash as Cinque measured out ten lashes on Kwong's back. Konnoma shouted from the batten. "Land! Many birds. There is land!" Turning in the breeze above the Amistad, two albatrosses were lifted in the current and glided on.

Late in the afternoon, off the Bahamas, a boat went ashore for water and whatever else could be found. Montez watched the happy group return to the ship. That night Montez again steered northwest to the United States.

The next morning a strong headwind blew from the east—with only one tattered sail the boat began to drift. Montez and Ruiz were asleep, chained to the deck. Cinque felt they were going backward, he yelled to throw out the anchor. Montez woke up. Half in English, half in Spanish, Montez tried to explain to Antonio, then to Cinque that "The anchor here is no good. There's no bottom."

"There is no bottom. It's not like a river." Ruiz added.

Cinque laughed, not believing him. Indignantly he glared at Montez. Antonio translated. "If there is a bottom, that lying Spaniard will lie no more."

Cinque ran his finger across his throat in a cutting motion. Montez knew the fear of the natives, the confusion of language, poor food, bad water, heat, and frustrations were bubbling just near the breaking point. Cinque ordered the anchor overboard and all watched the long chain rattle—clunk—to its end.

Cinque jumped overboard, grabbed the chain and pulled himself down following the chain to the anchor. Looking down past the anchor he could see no bottom. Swimming with all of his strength, lungs bursting, he finally broke through the surface. Gasping for air he climbed on deck, looked at the group amazed.

"No bottom!" he gasped.

CHAPTER THREE

August 24th, 1839

Montez and Ruiz lay on the deck, half covered under a canvas staring up at a circling petrel. Cinque was at the wheel. Antonio sat, staring at the horizon. Several Africans, Kimbo, Konnoma, and Bartu, fished with string over the side. Ruiz started to speak. Montez stopped him, nodding at Antonio. "In English. Antonio."

"Montez! We cannot keep zigging back and forth day and night. Day and night! We will die a hundred miles from safety."

"Hope for a man-of-war." Montez said hoarsely.

"That's your plan? Hope!? I feel better praying for the heavens to open and the flaming hand of God to shred their flesh and fry their blood."

"Very Christian. You think sailing to Africa is a better plan!? The sails are not just loose…they're shredded, food is low, six of your blacks have died, we at least are alive. If you have a secret plan, now's the time to reveal it."

Antonio sat up, pointed, and shouted in Mende just as one of the Africans in the crow's nest yelled down in Mende, "Land!"

The Africans argued, some pointed east, others west.

Montez stood and called to Antonio who ran over laughing.

"Ha, ha, ha! They think this could not be home, not enough days you know have passed. But, Kwong thinks maybe it could be some land between us and Africa."

They were off the coast of Long Island. Cinque, who had been scanning the horizon growled at Montez. Antonio translated.

"Cinque says: If this is a trick, the Spaniards will die."

A moonlit, tattered silhouette, the Amistad, crept towards Egg Harbor. Several merchant ships passed uninterested. Cinque ordered the two Spaniards below.

At sunrise the ship Eveline came alongside. Cinque, with an armed crew, waited for the Eveline to get close enough and shouted: "Food, water!"

Eveline's captain stared at what looked like The Lost Dutchman, manned by a nearly naked and fearful assortment of Africans. The captain looked through his glass. He mumbled to the first mate. "Judas priest! Sails in tatters, cargo barrels and crates scattered everywhere. A horrendous mess— to any proper New England skipper, that."

"The master of Eveline cautious." Antonio said as he translated for Cinque.

"Where ye bound?" the captain shouted into his horn.

"Africa!"

"Where be your captain?"

"Very sick."

"Stand to and we shall send over food and tow the ship to safe harbor."

Cinque motioned Montez on deck. The captain called to Montez thinking he might be the ship's captain. On first emotion, Montez shouted back in Spanish, then started to say something in English. Cinque stopped him. The Eveline's crew threw a towline with a grappling hook and tied the tow rope. Alarmed that they are being captured, Cinque and natives, armed with cane knives and muskets, fired on the Eveline.

The captain cut the line and sailed off.

"Back to Africa. Back to Africa!" Antonio nervously watched Cinque start a chant.

"Cinque, we must go ashore. We must get food. We must get water. There's gold of the captain in the cabin. Use it to buy provisions."

Next came the pilot boat, Blossom. The captain brought his vessel close by the starboard side and cast a tow line. Cinque appeared in the cabin door wearing only the captain's watch and chain, a compass, whip, sextant, and a snuff box tied around his waist. The two young sailors who had just jumped aboard glare at Cinque. What had they entered?

"The captain of the pilot boat Blossom sends greetings and asks the captain of the Amistad for his papers. Do you speak English?"

The first seaman glanced at a group of nearly naked Africans edging along the port side. Almost under his breath he said, "James—look."

James stood back, trying to keep eye contact with Cinque, who seemed in command as he walked out of the captain's quarters. James's voice was firm. "Where are you out of, where you bound? Do you need water? There is a doctor just there."

He pointed at a white saltbox by the shore. "Food? What happened here?" James nervously watched the motion of the group advancing toward him.

"Holy Mother—"

Thirty Africans with cane knives surrounded them on three sides. Silence. Then finally, edging nearer and nearer to the rail, the seamen panicked and leapt overboard shouting, "Captain, captain! Pirates, mutineers! Cannibals! Savages!"

They splashed to their dingy and made for their ship. Cinque couldn't understand the words, but he knew they were in danger. He commanded his men to fire. Blossom and Eveline took full sail to report to the navy.

Cinque watched the ships sail away, turned and pointed East, "Africa!"

Ruiz was exasperated, trying to keep his temper under control and negotiate was becoming more and more difficult. Cinque pivoted and entered the captain's cabin.

"Mother of God! At every turn fate is against us. Cinque, we must get more food and water."

Montez followed Cinque into the captain's cabin. Pointing at the map on the table he drew a short line to Block Island and showed Cinque where they were.

Ruiz showed Antonio and Antonio translated. "Block Island is our best hope for bartering some of the captain's gold doubloons for food. Here, see, and we will be away from those ships."

Montez uttered under his breath in English. "And a Man of War."

As night drew its curtain a stiff breeze blew in from the east and Gardiners Island came into view. Montez smiled and shouted at the three Africans on night duty with him. "More sail! More sail. Come on."

The African crew hoisted sail. Gardiners Island: he came as close to shore as he could navigate, then—Montez spun the wheel, caught the wind, and came about hard. So sudden was the turn that lines snapped, sails banged. Everyone and everything not tied down sprawled across the deck. Cinque ran across the deck and pulled Montez from the wheel. They barely missed going aground on a sandbar. Two slaves grabbed Montez and raised their cane knives. Cinque shouted "stop!" in Mende.

"We can no longer trust Montez. He must die, but after he is given trial by Mende law. But first—he was right we must get water and food."

Culloden Point, at the east side of Montauk, was named after H.M.S. Culloden, a British warship that ran aground in a gale in 1781. There were clear skies overhead with a little early morning mist as Antonio and five men from the Amistad rowed ashore.

Two white children playing with stick guns pushed through underbrush pretending to be scouts in Indian territory. One hiding from the others peeked up out of the underbrush and saw—Africans. They all jumped up and ran. Their mother laughed to herself as she heard the excited shouts of her boys. She hung the last of the laundry and turned to see what the excitement was about. The kids ran up the slope waving their arms, almost knocking her over. She laughed. They tugged at her. She scolded. They tugged. She turned to yell at them and saw a line of Blacks in rags walking up the hill.

Antonio had practiced asking for food in English over and over all the way from the boat. He knocked at the door. In acceptable English he asked, "Madam is the master of the house home? We would like to purchase some vegetables and maybe a few chickens or a pig." The double Dutch-door bottom bolted and the top held by a heavy chain edged open and a musket poked in Antonio's face. "Begone heathens or thou will meet thy maker sooner not later."

Hint taken, the group moved on down a wagon path, past fields of dried corn stalks, to the next farm. Women and children rushed indoors. Doors were bolted and windows shuttered at the sight of the Africans.

Since no one would talk to them and all the menfolk seemed to be working somewhere else they decided to just dig up vegetables and take pigs or chickens and negotiate later. Wandering from farm to farm they bickered amongst themselves about a proper price for these alien-looking pigs, and if those chickens were of a quality they were used to, and then argued amongst themselves what to pay for vegetables. Finally, after ten minutes debating the faults of a pig, they left two gold coins at the pig's stall. In an open field, the Africans feasted on potatoes and vegetables they foraged. Then dragged the squealing and kicking pig to the skiff.

That night Montez was led on deck by four Africans. Palaver started. Pans and barrels were used as drums. Chanting, shouting, pointing, the dancers danced around the accused. The children, always quiet, sat quietly watching. Cinque's court was primitive but direct. Each African stepped forward with an accusation in Mende. The verdict was death.

Montez was not young—the death tribunal with flashing knives, screams and threatening gestures emotionally broke him. The dance swirled on into the night. The sounds carried easily across the misty early morning bay as the sun broke the horizon.

Alien sounds echoed along shore like a rising tide. The rhythm beaten on the bottom of empty barrels. The words, an ancient chorus that called for spirits to guide the judgment of the tribunal. The chants punctuated the steady beat—decidedly human versions of high-pitched parrot calls, angry monkeys, and elephant trumpeting keep cadence with the stomping of feet and drums easily heard by those ashore. Montez lost count of how long the ritual circled him member by member shouting at him, but the sun was up. Then the dance stopped.

Montez, limp on the deck, softly cried Hail Mary's. Antonio smiled as he turned from Cinque, then looked appropriately sad as he slid across the deck and sat next to Montez.

"Cinque tell Antonio, tell Montez they not kill you on the ship. They do not want your spirit with them on the voyage to Africa. They keep you in chains. Like slaves below decks. When they are at sea, they will feed you to the sharks so spirit of Montez not harm them."

The next morning, Cinque and six Africans rowed across the quiet bay with just the soft sound of their oars, wind, and the distant sound of sea birds. Ashore they formed a line that snaked through barberry and sea grape, and a few tupelo trees along the wetlands. Prairie grasses — bluestem, skunk cabbage with huge, lush leaves the size of elephant ears, and Indian nut-grass covered much of their trek.

The further in they walked the louder the bird sound became—palm warbler, yellow warbler, tufted titmouse, cardinal, chickadee, crow, blue jay, white-throated sparrow, red-tailed hawk, turkey, woodpeckers, and gulls. Looking back into the disappearing mist, Montauk Point was about twelve miles beyond the ship. The southern shore of Napeague Harbor was maybe three miles. North was

Block Island Sound, south, the Atlantic Ocean. There was one cabin here, in the distance several lines of smoke rose from what were probably more houses.

A twelve-year-old boy digging in the garden yanked up a potato plant with four tubers caught in the roots. A hound rushed out of the underbrush barking and ran past the kid holding a hoe. He shook the tubers and shoved them in his basket, then looked up. Startled, he gaped at the group from the Amistad pushing through the long grass. He dropped his basket and ran full tilt around the corner of the house shouting. "Pa! Pa, Injuns, invaders, warrior party, Pa." *Slam!* The door banged shut. The muffled commotion from the house was hard to make out over the barking and the kid shouting at the top of his lungs.

Cinque cautiously walked around the front of the house to a weather—beaten door. He knocked, wanting to barter for the farmer's dog barking somewhere deep in the house.

The farmer smiled, standing behind the top of the half open Dutch door. He seemed friendly, accepted a gold coin. He bartered with the natives—a cocked pistol just behind his doorway. They wanted to barter him for the dog and for rum. The man shook his head and pointed to a pig pen. "No, no, not the dog, that pig over there. Understand? This will buy the pig. I have no use for rum. No. Rum."

Antonio nodded. The man put the coin in his pocket. Burna, and Konnoma walked to the pig pen bantering loudly and waving their arms about how they'll carry the huge animal.

"How come ye here? Where ye bound?" The farmer smiled.

Antonio points at the Amistad barely seen over a dune. "Sierra Leone, we going back!"

"White captain?"

"Black."

Antonio translated to Cinque who stood with his objects of authority around his waist, over an embroidered silk loincloth, his arms folded across his bare chest, his feet wide apart. He distrusted Whites. The farmer touched his forehead in a salute and closed and locked the door. The bargaining over, Cinque motioned they must leave.

At sunset a fire was started on the beach, the pig was butchered and skewered. The group laughed and told of their adventures to the group. Returning from washing blood off his hands in the bay, Pungwuni pointed at the farmer and two ships' captains who sat on horseback watching the beach party on the rise at the far end of their clearing. The Americans were each armed with pistols in their belts and rifles across their laps. The Mende scattered.

The three yelled for the Africans to stop, dismounted, and made a big show of putting their rifles on the ground. "Come back. We are in peace. Come. We want to help." Cinque grabbed Antonio's arm and advanced slowly. They recognized the farmer and stopped a dozen feet from him. The captains, Green and Fordham, smiled and

stood at ease scanning the group.

Captain Green pointed at Antonio. "Ask them about the gold, the doubloons?"

Fordham leaned close to the other captain and chuckled, "Don't be gettin' too pushy. Softly, softly." Then to Antonio, "This is free America, there are no slaves here."

Cinque looked at their dress, they wore captain's hats, and their coats and trousers were well made. "You are captains?"

"Aye," Green said, a little more loudly than necessary.

This interested Cinque, "You sail to Africa before?"

Fordham nodded, "Aye."

"Long time ago?"

Fordham laughed, "Aye. A while ago. But it's still in the same place isn't it." Antonio wasn't sure what he meant by that.

"You can take us there? We can pay you." Cinque added, "All the gold on the ship, three boxes, maybe eight thousand dollars. For you. You sail us to Africa."

The captains looked at each other—one unsaid thought. Green pointed to the ground as he said, "You bring the gold to the beach and we shall talk."

Cinque, in Mende, ordered Kagne to take two others and row to the ship and bring one of the trunks of money to shore. It took five minutes and the dingy was bobbing alongside the *Amistad*. Kagne scampered over the rails and ran to the captain's cabin. Four Africans standing guard peppered him with questions all at once. He hoisted a chest to his shoulder and hurried across the deck.

As he climbed the Amistad's railing, they sighted a sail east on the horizon. Worried, they hurried down the ladder, almost dropped the chest, jumped into the dingy, and rowed furiously to shore. The captains were also looking long at the horizon and recognized the silhouette if the USS Washington. (Not named after George Washington, but for Peter G. Washington, who was Assistant Secretary of the treasury).

The Africans preparing their feast stopped as Kwong pointed at the new ship growing fast on the horizon.

Green swore. "Ah, Jesus, it's the war brig Washington, out of New York."

Cinque splashed to the Amistad dingy with several Africans to grab the trunk and bring the skid ashore.

The two captains stepped away from the rest and struck a plan. "These must be the blacks mentioned in The Sag Harbor Corrector. They called them Pirates! Pha! Buccaneers, and bloody slave mutineers? I tell you Green, They's a bunch of scared children."

Fordham laughed. "Lookin' for the impossible is what they are. Sail to Africa?! I sez damn them. I sez, capture the Blacks, take the doubloons and the ship. Turn the bloody mutineers over to the customs people and you an' me, we splits the reward."

CHAPTER FOUR

August 26th, 1839

The USS Washington's captain stood by the starboard bow ratlines focusing his telescope as several junior officers clustered around him. He pivoted and gave the order, "Board that derelict and see if they are in distress." Marines and crew were piped on deck. The Washington dropped anchor. A well-ordered drill of marines and an officer disembarked on a pinnace.

Lieutenant Gedney saw a number of people on the beach with carts, horses, and a dingy passing to and fro—he was the officer on board the cutter sent to board the Amistad. On coming along side, a number of Negroes were discovered on her deck, and twenty or thirty more were on the beach. Six Marines bounded onto the deck, sabers and pistols drawn and formed a battle line. Fierce-looking Konoma, with a leg bone of a pig in one hand and a machete in the other, his teeth filed to a point, led a brief attack on the boarding party. But the Africans were no match for armed marines trained in close-quarter fighting.

Ruiz, hearing the shouting and screaming, ran on deck, babbled incoherently in English and Spanish as the marines bound the subdued Africans. "This is my ship, my slaves! They are killers, savages—more are on the beach."

Montez managed to drag his chains topside and fell to the deck laughing. The lieutenant ordered the tattered Spanish flag raised. Lieutenant Gedney pointed at the flag man and ordered him, "Signal the Washington to send another long-boat ashore."

In crisp quick moves, the wigwag was sent to the Washington. Almost immediately two longboats were lowered and underway.

The sound of the brief and loud fight on the Amistad reverberated over the water and was heard as if it were on shore. Cinque and the natives ran to their boat to aid the Amistad, then seeing two boats from the Washington—with men and arms, they turned back for shore. A cannon shot was fired; the ball splashed twenty feet in front of the crowded Africans' pinnace. Cinque and the others splashed ashore and ran for the captains. Antonio fell before them pleading for help.

The marines landed. Navy Lieutenant Meade waded ashore with his men, who surrounded Cinque and the captains, and arrested the remaining slaves. Capt. Green tried to bluster past a marine's bayoneted rifle to argue with Lt. Meade. He had no luck with that. More Africans were brought in from the dunes by four marines.

The captains and Cinque hovered over the chest of gold. Lt. Gedney ordered his men to watch them all and instructed his flag man: "Tell the Washington we have thirty-two Africans and three Americans on the beach. Advise."

The two captains and the farmer who stood in front of the chest of gold were furious at the intrusion of their business transaction and threatened to sue the lieutenant, the Washington's captain, the U.S. Navy, and the US government. They were captains and were laws unto themselves on their ships. But this argument didn't seem to work against the U.S. Navy.

Cinque didn't know English but pleaded with the two captains to save them.

Stern-faced, the three Montauks turned to the lieutenant and demand:

"This trunk and others shipboard are ours. We rescued them, we claim them as salvage."

Lieutenant Gedney pointed his pistol at the captains and waved them to the long boat.

"You will accompany us, gentlemen. Then you can make your claim to the Navy."

"Our horses?"

"If you hadn't claimed salvage and made legal claims, I could have let you go. But now that's the captain of the Washington's prerogative to make those decisions—hopefully your horses will understand."

On August 29th, 1839—The 190 ton, 91 foot, 10 gun, USS Washington, was anchored in New Haven harbor: The first Amistad trial was on the USS Washington.

The Washington first set sail on 6 July 1837. Her assignment was to conduct "winter cruising" off the Virginia capes and New York, where she spotted the Amistad and took it in tow. The USS Washington's captain's cabin comfortably held the dozen men who opened the first trial of the Amistad.

A dozen ships sailed close by—all tacking in the light breeze. A dozen ships' s curious crews and passengers stood by their rails looking at the Africans on the USS

Washington's deck. The Africans, in chains, were watched closely by armed marines who stood at the ready. A line from the stern of the USS Washington was taut as it pulled against the beaten and battered 200 ton, 120 foot Amistad that had tattered sails, broken mast, and was manned by a skeleton crew from the Washington. The crew downed sail and watched as the marshal, judge, several aides, and guests were piped aboard the Washington. The resulting trials became the focus building on all the other problems that had been churning in America.

Even before this trial began the trunks of gold disappeared, never to be seen again, but with the salvage laws of the sea being what they were there were several civilian claims to the gold. Two navy officers, the U.S. Navy, Cuba, the Spanish government, and the US government, all petitioned for the gold—even Gedney, Meade, Ruiz, and Montez applied since they said they had helped rescue the ship's cargo and helped capture the Africans.

The captain waited for all to be seated and nodded to the court officer.

"Lt. Meade will translate your honor."

A rum libation was passed around for court officers to brighten their tea. When he was offered rum, the Judge shook his head and pointed to Ruiz. "Senor Don Jose Ruiz will be sworn."

Lt. Meade faced Don Jose and swore him in—in Spanish. Senior Ruiz was a bit inhibited by the power that surrounded him. The ship, the judge and the captain, were all American and he had had troubles with the US Navy since the American government outlawed the sale of slaves in 1807. Don Jose spoke hesitantly in Spanish. Lt. Meade translated.

"I bought 49 slaves in Havana, and shipped them on board the schooner Amistad. We sailed for Guanaja, the intermediate port for Principe. For the four first days everything went well. Then, in the night I heard a noise in the forecastle. All of us were trying to sleep, except the man at the helm. I do not know how things began, but I was awakened by the noise. This man Joseph, I saw. I could not tell how many were engaged. There was no moon. It was very dark. Sea spray and rain made the deck slippery in the heavy ocean."

Don Jose Ruiz said hesitantly, "Without a weapon I took up an oar and tried to quell the mutiny. I cried 'No! NO!' I then heard one of the crew cry murder. I heard the captain order the cabin boy to go below, and I called Montez to follow me. Then I saw the captain, struggling, with difficulty, trying to pull his blade out of a slave. The battle was hard to see in the night. Footing was hard to keep you know, the ocean-pounding the deck. Africans streamed on deck.

Then more and more slaves released their chains and grabbed machetes. The ship wallowed as wave after wave broke over the cabin. I grabbed Montez and we were chased across the deck into the hold. There, in total darkness, we crashed into broken crates and cargo, I managed to squeeze into a shallow storage bin. Montez dived under some canvas behind stacked barrels.

"A dozen Africans, shouting back and forth in three different African dialects I didn't know, searched the flooded storage area with torches. Montez and I were pulled from hiding and dragged on deck where Cinque stopped the slaves from killing the two of us. I told them not to kill me, I did not see the captain killed. The one called Cinque called me on deck and told me I should not be hurt. The ship was floundering. I told them it would sink unless I took the wheel.

"They tied Montez's hands. We were kept on the bloodied deck. The slaves told us the next day they had killed all but the cabin boy, who said three had escaped. I think they would have killed him, but he acted as interpreter between us, as he understood some Spanish and some Mende."

Ruiz looked at his guards; feeling he had said enough, he sat down. The Court officer glanced at Montez and said to officer Meade: "Senior Don Pedro Montez will be sworn. Lt. Meade will translate."

Montez looked from the bible to Ruiz as he was being sworn in. Montez lowered his hand and sat looking at the judge. Lieutenant Meade stood at parade rest with no emotion showing. Personally he did not believe in slavery. He would not be a slave. But this case was proving dangerous as evidenced by the arguments within his family. However, slavery was the law. The judge asked Montez to continue.

"We left Havana on the twenty-eighth of June. I owned four slaves, three females and a male. For three days the wind was ahead, and all went well. Between eleven and twelve at night, just as the moon was rising, the sky was dark and cloudy, the weather turned very rainy, rough. On the fourth night I laid down on a mattress. Between three and four I was awakened by a noise which I think was caused by blows given to the cook. I went on deck, and they attacked me. I seized a stick and a knife to defend myself. I did not wish to kill or hurt them. I was wounded on the head, severely with one of the sugar knives, also on the arm.

"I ran below and stowed myself between two barrels wrapped in a sail. One of the prisoners prevented the men from killing me. I was faint from loss of blood. I was taken on deck and strapped by the hand to him, Antonio, the cabin boy."

"Lt. Meade will give the oath to Antonio."

Antonio looked around the huge ship and smiled as the lieutenant swore him in.

Antonio spoke in Spanish and was translated by Meade.

"I am a Christian, sí."

"Do you swear to tell the whole truth and nothing but the truth, so help you God?"

Antonio nodded, started his statement, but stopped as a cabin boy entered with a tray with tea. The judge pointed at his desk and nodded. He took out his tote and poured a healthy dram. Antonio continued. "I do. We had been out four days when the mutiny broke out. That night it had been raining very hard, and all hands rushed on deck. The rain stayed, it was very dark. Clouds covered the moon. Four of the slaves came aft, armed with those knives used to cut sugar cane. They cut me."

Lt. Gedney stood at parade rest and delivered his rehearsed speech to the court. "While the U.S. Brig Washington was sounding, August 26th, 1839, between Gardiner's and Montauk Points, a schooner was seen lying in shore off Culloden Point, under circumstances so suspicious as to authorize to stand in to see what was her character."

As the trial rejoined, a cabin boy on deck rattled a newspaper, ran his finger across the print, and read to another young man by the rail. "Lookit here, John

Greenleaf Whittier, says right here, 'William S. Hollabird attorney for the United States, a Van Buren man, set the hearing aboard the USS Washington. U.S. district Judge Judson, a Van Buren appointee, found the slaves guilty and commanded that they be tried in circuit court in Hartford.' What is the world coming to Thomas?"

The USS Washington's captain's cabin was large by ship's standards, but not meant as a courtroom. All filed in and settled facing the captain's desk. The U.S. Marshal scanned the room and cleared his throat.

"Ahem. All upstanding! His Honor Andrew T. Judson, U.S. District Judge for the bench. MR.C.A. Ingersoll, Esq. You are appearing for the U.S. District Attorney?"

"Yes."

"Let the minutes so state."

"Lt. Gedney you are still under oath." The judge looks up from his notes.

"Yes sir."

"Please continue."

Cinque was brought into the captain's cabin manacled, wearing a red flannel shirt, navy issue duck pantaloons, and a snuff box around his neck. He had used this ploy to make the Mende recognize him as chief—it was not working here.

Glancing at his notes briefly, Lieutenant Gedney explained to the court the background of the case.

"The schooner proved to be the Amistad, Capt. Ramon Flues, from Havana, bound for Guanaja, Port Principe, with sixty Blacks and two passengers on board. The vessel was steered for the Island of St. Andrews, near New Providence—from thence she went to Green Key, where the Blacks laid in a supply of water."

USS Washington's Deck
August 29th, 1839

Ruiz sat smoking a long dark Havana on deck. Serenely, every now and then he clasped his hands, and with uplifted eyes, gave thanks again to the Holy Virgin for his deliverance. Waiting on deck, the Washington's quartermaster listened to Lt. Gedney as he paused and lit a clay pipe. Gedney leaned against a twelve pounder by the main deck boat skids, pointed at Ruiz, "Both those Spaniards were thankful for their deliverance. Jose Pedro is the most striking instance of complacency and unalloyed delight I have ever witnessed. And, not strange, he said it was only yesterday he was sentenced to death by the chief of the buccaneers, with his death song chanted for hours by that crew, all of them dancing, and yelling and swinging those machetes all around."

September 1839

Weaving in and out of the horses and carriages on the busy New Haven street, the Africans were escorted to the jail by the Marshal. People stopped and quietly stared. The Africans stared back at them. The town was full of shops and shoppers, women in feathered hats and long dresses were covered from their neck to their shoes. Along the street many of the buildings were five-story brick and stone with 90 degree sharp corners and all had many windows, now that king George didn't get a tax on windows. There were towers and steeples, stores of every imaginable sort, block after block. The natives were fascinated by the strange land and strange customs of the people who lived here.

Philadelphia's new modern natural gas light glared through the words THE PENNSYLVANIA FREEMAN PRESS—JOHN GREENLEAF WHITTIER ~ PROPRIETOR inscribed in gold on the window. Two men worked the large black printing press setting type. Whittier proof-read out loud as the press was being inked. Two other sweaty men strained pushing a heavy stack of paper; another cut binding string while a printer's devil broke apart frames of wooden type, sorted and threw the type into bins expertly without looking, knowing by heart the order of the type tray. The type setter watched Whittier and awaited instructions, then quickly type set his corrections. Whittier had been trained as a cobbler, aware that every shoe had a fit, that like the people who wore them one pair of shoes was not exactly like another. This philosophy made its way into his thinking about people and the world. Otherwise he was a poet. His friends William Cullen Bryant, Ralph Waldo Emerson, Henry Wadsworth Longfellow, James Russell Lowell, Mark Twain, and Oliver Wendell Holmes knew him as an abolitionist who was lucky to be alive because of beliefs he broadcast.

Mumbling over the last few sentences of copy Whittier finally said: "There were no African interpreters at the trial. The Africans had no legal counsel. The Africans were transported to the New Haven—fail? That's a J not an F. Which turned into a circus, hundreds of people a day are paying two cents each to see caged African pyrates. Pi not Py. Three of the Africans died there of dysentery. Di, not dy". Referring to the paper he held, he nodded. "That looks better. Keep them coming! Charles, tell the boys on the street, be ready in half an hour."

"But don't let the little hooligans inside," griped one of the paper cutters.

The typesetter laughed. "Ah they're good lads—when they're not in jail."

Just before day broke a pack of scruffy street kids snapped up packets of *The Independent* as they hit the floor. Ink still wet, they cut the bindings and ran into the streets hawking their own made up more exciting headlines, full voice.

"Pirates captured!"

"Navy crushes slave revolt!"

"Bloody battle at Culloden Point! Christianity safe."

"American shores safe from African pirates."

CHAPTER FIVE

Supreme Court
February 24th, 1841

It was a cold and windy Washington day; trees stood darkly in the misty morning, a promise of leaf buds dotting their branches. Inside the courtroom was "that damned Adams," the fighter. Old John Quincy Adams, politician, diplomat, lawyer, sixth president of the United States, who spoke nine languages, weighed in at two hundred, and two pounds, a sturdy Massachusetts farmer with a cutting wit, five feet seven inches tall, bald, with long bushy white sideburns, and perpetually disapproving knitted brows, he was the prime contender for most vexatious man on the senate floor. This day his voice echoed around the courtroom as he scanned the crowd.

"It is, peculiarly painful to me, under present circumstances, to be under the necessity of arraigning before this court and before the civilized world, the course of the existing administration in this case. But I must do it."

There was standing room only and the packed room was overheated with the bodies of spectators. There was no Supreme Court Building, the court used space in the new Capitol Building, later moving half a dozen times around the Capitol. The weather rattled against the windows that were partly open to circulate fresh air. Sounds of iron wheels and horse hoofs on cobbles clattered around the room. A band of six anti-abolitionist blackface musicians cavorted and played "Knock a Nigger Down." Street hawkers sold food and papers to the curious gathered on the street, lawn, and courthouse steps. The courtroom's gold gilded eagle was barely seen in shadow.

Clouds tried to hold back the sun; two lamplighters circled the large room. Adams, thumbs hooked under his suspenders, paced as he began his nearly nine-hour defense. "That the government is still in power, and thus, subject to the control of the court, the lives and liberties of all my clients are in its hands. And if I should pass over the course it has pursued, those who have not had an opportunity to examine the case and perhaps the court itself, might decide that nothing improper had been done and that the parties I represent had not been wronged by the course pursued by the executive."

Large milling crowds tried to push into the outer chambers of the crowded court. Students stood shoulder to shoulder in the crowded back of the court they called the balcony. You couldn't buy entertainment like this, but wealthy men and women paid under the table to sit in pews in the main room. Reporters and artists lined the first two rows to one side. A group of students who started a waiting line before daybreak saw a fashion plate of a banker bribe a guard at the entrance. They pointed and started a chant of "Shame, shame, shame." A dozen other students upstairs joined in, not knowing why repeated it. The court officer scowled, shaking his truncheon at them threateningly. That didn't work.

The crowd murmured wondering who the Marine guards were escorting in. Ruiz and Montez, who were on the Amistad, were gentlemen plantation owners, who for their day in court were powered, perfumed, and in their finest attire. They scanned the crowd nervously. Congressman TH Benton of Mississippi scowled at Adams and poked an associate angrily. "It's not *what* Adams says, damn his eyes! It's *how* he says it! He's so damn caustic, he could recite Little Bo Peep and you'd want to lynch her."

Adams pivoted dramatically and glared at the prosecution. "All the proceedings of the government, Executive and Judicial, in this case have been founded on the—assumption—that the two Spanish slave-dealers were the only parties aggrieved. That all the right was on their side, and all the wrong on the side of their surviving self-emancipated victims.

"I ask your honors, was this justice? No. It was not so considered by Mr. Forsyth himself. He calls it 'sympathy,' and he so calls it because from the very first intervention of Lt. Gedney he says:"—Adams reads from a document—"Messrs. Ruiz and Montez were first found near the coast of the United States, deprived of their property and their freedom, suffering from lawless violence on their persons, and in imminent and constant danger of being deprived of their lives also.

"They were found in this distressing and perilous situation by officers of the United States, who, moved towards them by sympathetic feeling which subsequently became as it were national. Immediately rescued them from personal danger, restored them to freedom, secured their oppressors that they might abide the consequences of the acts of violence perpetrated upon them, and placed under the safeguard of the laws all the property which they claimed as their own..."

The courtroom was packed. Open windows let in a little air and a lot of outside confusion that built as the day went on. A row of uniformed navy officers from the Washington and a few who were involved in transporting the Africans from the ship sat at attention by the entrance. Their only motion was their eyes following Adams who paced the front of the court.

The actor in Adams paused, remembering which delivery for which phrase he had practiced. "This sympathy with Spanish slave-traders is declared by the Secretary to have been first felt by Lieutenant Gedney. I hope this is not correctly represented. It is imputed to him and declared to have been a national sympathy. A national sympathy with slave-traders? Of the barracoons? Officially declared to be the prime motive of action of the government: And this fact is given as an answer to all the claims, demands and reproaches of the Spanish minister! The sympathy of the Executive government, and—as it were, of the nation, in favor of the slave-traders, and against these poor, unfortunate, helpless, tongue-less, defenseless, Africans, was the cause and foundation and motive of all these proceedings and has brought this case up for trial before your honors."

Two newspaper artists in the front row, Clay and Atkin, quickly sketched the crowd, capturing the energy of the room. They did exaggerate their sketches of arguments between abolitionists and southern slaveholders, wild-eyed protesters shouting, kicking over spittoons, fists flying, some were seated, some smoked, some chewed with expressions ranging from disgust to anger to frivolity. Maybe they were a bit exaggerated, but emotionally, close to true. It was a carnival for the artists. One played with the scowl of the judge, another sketches Montez line by line exaggerating his deadpan courtroom face. They each flipped over to a fresh page and covered it with the myriad of emotions churning through the worry of the courtroom's attitudes.

There was back and forth vocal support among the students who had to be shushed several times during the trial. That didn't work. Still nervous, the slaves didn't really understand what was happening around them. The language was still strange to them, and the bellowing of pro- and anti-abolition groups inside and outside the courtroom was as animalistic as any jungle sonance. The guards glared at the Africans—weapons at the ready. The judge was antagonistic to both groups. The lawyer for Montez and Ruiz shouted above the clamor and pushed his way through the crowded courtroom to present his writ for the ownership of the slaves. The two officers from the ship USS Washington jumped up to protest demanding the slaves and ship as salvage under the law of the sea.

A chorus of students in the hall set up a chant, "Blood money, Blood money, Blood money." Barely heard, a student in the balcony started singing a new American song, *My Country, 'tis of Thee*. Two more voices started in and then all the students joined. Written in 1831 by a student, Francis Smith. It used the melody of the British royal anthem.

Some in the packed room turned to glare at the students, others smiled.

"Sweet Land. Land where my fathers died,
Land of the pilgrims' pride,
From every mountain side let Freedom ring.
My native country, thee,
Land of the noble free,
Thy name I love;
I love thy rocks and rills,
Thy woods and templed hills,
My heart with rapture thrills Like that above.

Our fathers' God to Thee,
Author of Liberty,
To thee we sing,
Long may our land be bright
With Freedom's holy light,
Protect us by thy might Great God, our King."

The judge banged his gavel and pointed at the students. This time they quieted. The district courts judge stunned the Van Buren administration. It ruled that because the Amistad rebels had been born free, they could not be treated as property, and must be returned to Africa. Van Buren's district attorney, Gilpin, appealed the verdict to the Circuit Court, which upheld the District Court's decision. The case then went to the U.S. Supreme Court.

John Forsyth, then Secretary of State wrote: "It is true, by the treaty between Great Britain and Spain, the slave trade is prohibited to the subjects of each; but the parties to this treaty or agreement are the proper judges of any infraction of it, and they have created special tribunals to decide questions arising under the treaty; nor does it belong to any other nation to adjudicate upon it, or to enforce it... In the case of the ship Antelope, (10 Wheaton, page 66), this subject was fully examined, and the opinion of the Supreme Court of the United States establishes the following points:

1. That, however unjust and unnatural the slave trade may be, it is not contrary to the law of nations.
2. That, having been sanctioned by the usage and consent of almost all civilized nations, it could not be pronounced illegal, except so far as each nation may have made it so by its own acts or laws; and these could only operate upon itself, its own subjects or citizens; and, of course, the trade would remain lawful to those whose Government had not forbidden it.
3. That the right of bringing in and adjudicating upon the case of a vessel charged with being engaged in the slave trade, even where the vessel belongs to a nation which has prohibited the trade, cannot exist. The courts of no country execute the penal laws of another...

In the case now before me, the vessel is a Spanish vessel, belonging exclusively to Spaniards, navigated by Spaniards, and sailing under Spanish papers and flag, from one Spanish port to another. It therefore follows, unquestionably, that any offence committed on board is cognizable before the Spanish tribunals, and not elsewhere.

These two points being disposed of—1st. That the Government of the United States is to consider these Negroes as the property of the individuals in whose behalf the Spanish minister has put up a claim; 2d. That the United States cannot proceed against them criminally;— the only remaining inquiry is, what is to be done with the vessel and cargo? the Negroes being part of the latter.

"The claimants of these Negroes have violated none of our laws... They have not come within our territories with the view or intention of violating the laws of the United States... They have not introduced these Negroes into the United Sates for the purpose of sale, or holding them in servitude within the United States. It therefore appears to me that this subject must be disposed of upon the principles of international law and the existing treaties between Spain and the United States.

"These Negroes are charged with an infraction of the Spanish laws; therefore, it is proper that they should be surrendered to the public functionaries of that Government, that if the laws of Spain have been violated, they may not escape punishment. These Negroes deny that they are slaves; if they should be delivered to the claimants, no opportunity may be afforded for the assertion of their right to freedom. For these reasons, it seems to me that a delivery to the Spanish minister is the only safe course for this Government to pursue."

But many conflicts aggravated the word freedom at this time: Louis Tappan and his family had been attacked since the thirties for his Abolitionist stand. His house was burned in New York. He printed thousands of hand bills and sent them in the US mail across the country. Three thousand angry racists in Charleston smashed into the U. S. Post Office. Then the mob of Charleston Christians gathered to burn the flyers and hang effigies of Tappan and other abolitionists. A fifty-thousand-dollar reward was offered for Tappan's by a Louisiana man. Anti-abolitionist leaders and southern newspapers demanded governors, and attorney generals to extradite, try, and hang Tappan and other members of the American Anti-slavery Society.

On September 4th, 1839 Louis Tappan, reverend Leavitt, and reverend Jocelyn, formed the *Amistad Committee,* and secured Roger Baldwin, Seth Staple, and Theodore Sedgwick, as legal counsel. While this was happening, America reacted to the hyperbole of newspapers North, East, West, and South, about *the Amistad.* Also, because a lot more was going on in their world Americans were not untroubled. For instance:

Lyman Beecher's book tour for *Plea for the West* 1835, about a Catholic plot to take over the U.S. incited mobs to set fire to Catholic schools. In Philadelphia gun battles broke out between "Americans" and Irish Catholics.

In 1835 Mexican soldiers attempted to disarm the inhabitants of Gonzales Texas, who refused to give up their cannon, sparked the first battle in the war for Texican independence. Then Sam Houston defeated Santa Ana at San Jacinto bringing an immediate end to hostilities.

Thousands of Americans died during the second Seminole War from 1835 to 1842. Gen. Thomas S. Jessup proclaimed it—"Not an Indian war but a negro war,"—a bit of merchandising that frightened the south, worried about two and a half million slaves rising up. Jessup was facing only three thousand Seminole warriors but could not win a battle. Under a flag of truce, during peace talks, his U.S. troops seized and arrested the Native American Seminole Chief, Osceola in Florida—who later died in jail in North Carolina. Jessup's underhanded maneuver outraged the American public when it hit the newspapers. Though no peace treaty was ever signed both Van Buren and Jackson were behind Jessup's actions.

The 1838 Mormon War. Missouri governor, Lilburn Boggs ordered all Mormons expelled from the state—

or exterminated—after they attacked a state authorized militia thinking it was an anti-Mormon mob. America was new and fertile ground for religions who came to escape prejudice and persecution in Europe. Anglicans, or Church of England, claimed Virginia; Massachusetts took in Puritans; New York city took in Jews; Pennsylvania got the Quakers; Baptists tithed in Rhode Island; and Roman Catholics took Maryland, Muslims were everywhere as slaves from Africa.

But religious wars were not only the province of the old world. Agitation and turmoil followed religious emigrants to the new world. Some states abolished certain churches and supported others. Many states issued preaching licenses; others collected tax money to establish state churches. Each state's constitution supported their own religion. After 1789 the First Amendment, in theory, was supposed to do away with religious prejudices.

Protestants in Massachusetts burned down a Catholic convent in 1834.

Then in 1838 there were the Battles of Crooked River, the Bear River massacre, the Bleeding Kansas battles, Utah War, Black Hawk War, Seminole Wars, Date Massacre, Battle of Horseshoe Bend, Battle of New Orleans, Tippecanoe—naming just a few disharmonies.

Then New York City banks ran out of gold and silver. They suspended payments in gold and wouldn't redeem commercial paper at face value.

A collapsing land bubble, and falling cotton prices led to Panic of '37—that led to the economic depression between 1839 and 1843, causing the holdings of American banks to drop by almost fifty percent—and closing many banks.

Then there was the burgeoning outrageous number of 17,000,000 Americans in 1830, and more "new Americans" arriving every day and heading out to the ever expanding borders. Besides Texas, presidents Madison, Monroe, Jackson, Van Buren, and Polk wanted California, Montana, Nevada, Idaho, Utah, New Mexico, most of Arizona, Colorado, parts of Oklahoma, Kansas, and Wyoming to become slave states.

This caused an enormous strain between the North and South.

It was a time, in America, when doctors were starting to go to school to study medicine as a science. Dr. Jenner came out of the cow barn where he discovered a cure for smallpox in 1796, other than smallpox, it was a task just surviving diseases in the 1800s anywhere. In addition to everything else, medicine and doctors were just becoming nearly reliable in a world full of war, sickness, and politicians. In 1830 nearly 30,000 Americans died of cholera. Consumption, tuberculosis, or white plague caused more deaths around the world than any other disease. Nearly 50 thousand died in America between 1830 and 1840; countless others barely survived or were never cured.

In 1837 the smallpox epidemic of California and the Pacific Northwest killed more than 17,000 people just along the Missouri River, and tens of thousands more native Blackfoot, Assiniboine, Arikara, Crow, and Pawnee died. Smallpox may have killed as much as 90% of all native population.

In 1838 Syphilis was fatal to two hundred and fifty or more white Americans. Uncounted tens of thousands of Native Americans died of this and other European diseases that they had no resistance against.

Thrush killed thousands in Delaware, Maryland, District of Columbia, Virginia, Tennessee, Kentucky, and North Carolina, California, Oregon and Washington, Missouri, and the Ohio river.

Then there was a multitude of nearly known or unknown deceases: Scurvy, tetanus, scrofula, tumors, brain inflammation, Saint Vitus dance, convulsions, and alcoholism, to name a few.

From just 1837-1840 over seventy thousand Americans died of diseases of the lungs: Quinsy, diphtheria, croup, laryngitis, whooping-cough. More than ten thousand died of Dysentery. Typhoid fever killed 6,000 Americans. Typhus killed 7,000 Americans. Measles was fatal to nearly 3,000 people in America. Pneumonia killed over twenty thousand in America. Just a few of the problems on the minds of America as the trial of the Amistad went to court.

CHAPTER SIX

February 24th, 1841 4:57 AM

Antoine had been in Adams's service for all the years Adams was in Washington. Antoine spoke with a French accent. Today, like every day, in Adams's Washington apartment, he placed Adams's vest, trousers, and jacket in a traveling basket and walked through the dining room, disappeared into the kitchen, and checked that breakfast was in the process of being prepared by the cook.

"It's good Mrs. Adams wasn't here for yesterday's court *chamaillerie.* The, how you say squabble."

"She does prefer the farm animals to politicians."

"My God, I hope never—or expect to see another day like yesterday."

The clock sounded five bells as Adams reached for the door. Antoine opened the door. Perfect timing from knowing Mr. A's habitual routine. After breakfast Antoine carried the basket outside; it was fifty degrees, a brisk wind blew from the Potomac. Adams wore a long coat and his boots were highly polished. He and Antoine walked to the waiting carriage. Antoine carefully placed the basket in the carriage. Adams walked briskly up the street. Antoine climbed up next to the smiling footman, Joseph. Jeremy,

Adam's free black coachman, lightly snaps the reins; the horses perk up and follow Adams, as he turns for the river.

"Umm, hmm you had a day I hear." Jeremy said. Like birds taking flight Antoine's *patois* uses his hands as much as his words. "Outside the court were speech makers, you know, and all those slave-hawks pushed into the yard, and there were drums beating, colors flying, and they all rush in to capture the speakers stand, you know. And shouting down the Abolitionists. They was nose punching, shin kicking, pate whacking and all tokens of vigorous physical resentments. Libertines inside and out. The Judge is inside the court. Ah! But the lawn was milling with crowds of people, behaving like so many—how you would say—Kilkenny cats. Old-school Democrats, New-school Democrats, and the rest calling each other names I never heard. The newspaper hawkers are no better, all manner of abuse and invectives with all the scrimmaging and hubbub, making up stories not even in the papers. There was pie-men, oyster-men, hot-chestnut men, cheese mongers, beer men, hot-muffin men, cake women and other vendors all bawling out their wares at the top of their lungs, yes, a real deafening din, and the Quaker women circulating, handing out their pamphlets."

Adams walked briskly across a lawn to the river where the mist was slowly rising. The coach followed. Adams had been talking to himself the entire time, repeating the same phrase over and over, rehearsing it with different emphasis, gesturing with his arms, reaching for the penetrating tone of a favorite actor, Edwin Forrest or Junius Brutus Booth who rolled their r's a bit too much, but who could be understood in the last row of the balcony of the National theatre.

They passed a carriage and two tradesmen's vans, both smiled and nodded. They knew Adams and his morning ritual.

Adams recited the same phrase waving his arms dramatically as he walked to the river. Otherwise, it was quiet.

"The *seizure* of the vessel, with the arrest and examination—The seizure of the vessel, with the *arrest* and examination—arrest *and* examination of the Africans was intended for inquiry, and to lead to an investigation of the rights of all parties. And consequently it now appears that everything ... everything which has flowed from this mistaken or misapplied sympathy," Adams paused and started again, emphasizing different words.

Steam rose off the river as finches and sparrows set up a chorus; a double-crested cormorant scooted across the Delaware. Antoine talked as he looked back and forth along the street to see if anyone was following. No one. He continued, "Buglers, fifers, drummers, bells, hand-bill stuffers, all sorts and conditions of men, jostling, you know, shoving, pushing, treading on one another's toes. It is some hurly-burly, you know. Not a few plug-uglies pushing folks deliberately—except around the soldiers. And there were few enough of them."

Would Adams retire from public service after Jackson was elected president? Not hardly. Adams easily won election to the House of Representatives, and served from 1831 to his death in 1848, joined the Anti-Masonic Party, switched to the Whig Party, which united the anti-President Jackson opposition.

Adams was never a slave holder—and while he was in Congress he became more and more antagonistic to the Southern slavers who controlled the Democratic Party. Adams knew the southern bloc's plan was to annex Texas and extend slavery by way of creating a Mexican-American war. Fighting the Jackson clique he led the repeal of the "gag rule" that prevented the House from debating any petition they chose. Congress, history, friend and foe—all agreed, Adams had a sharp mind, sharper tongue, was a great secretary of state, an unmatched diplomat, but not a great president. His problem? He had a grand agenda but no support in Congress.

Adams walked along the riverbank. The grass underfoot was cold and wet from the morning dew. He stopped and looked both ways. He looked back at Antoine standing on the coachman's seat surveying the field. Antoine nodded. Adams slipped off his boots and dropped his overcoat. Naked, he dove into the Potomac River. The carriage waited in the early morning brume as John Quincy Adams swam with long strokes going with the flow of the river, then flipped to a back stroke while reciting his speech.

"—which has flowed from this mistaken or misapplied *sympathy*, was wrong from the beginning. By what right all this *sympathy*, from Lt. Gedney to the Secretary of State, to the nation… By *what* right… By what right was it *denied* to the men who had restored themselves to freedom, and secured their oppressors? gasp! Ahhhhh! GOD! THIS IS COLD! But—the soul endeavors Lord. The soul endeavors."

March 1st, 1841

Proletarian and plebeian crowds alike agreed, this gathering was better than a circus side show. The gold gilded eagle, on the wall over the judge, cast long early morning shadows. Adams dourly surveyed the court, turned and started.

At times the outside rattles from street venders, carriages, pickets, and band music added to the drama of the case causing the prosecution to pause, or the defense to bellow out their indignation.

"When the Amistad first came within the territorial jurisdiction of the United States, acts of violence had passed between the two parties, the Spaniards and the Africans on board of her, but on which side these acts were lawless lies the question of right and wrong. If the government and people of the United States interfere at all, they are bound in duty to extend their sympathy to all; and if they intervened at all between them it must be not in sympathy, but Justice—dispensing to every individual— his own right."

The Boston docks were the second largest in America and battling to be first. They were loud and crowded as Charles Francis Adams and his wife arrived in an expensive coach with a driver and footman. They stopped at the gangplank of a packet for Washington DC. The footman jumped down from the back, lowered the carriage stairs, and opened the door. Charles stepped down, and turned to help his wife.

Abigail Brown Brooks' father was one of the wealthiest men in America, a shipping magnate, and president of the New England Insurance Company. The first footman hefted two suitcases and a trunk to two longshoremen who ran up the gangplank. Charles was annoyed as they boarded and made their way across the crowded deck. The lieutenant, knowing who they were, smiled and tipped his hat.

"Mr. and Mrs. Adams, welcome aboard."

Charles leaned to his wife and under his breath whispered. "It will–not–work. I'll say it again—Once

Father sets his mind to a thing. You know how he is; and with the uproar in congress, and the threats against his life, well, father's even more pig-headed than Grandfather, if that's possible."

"Then you have to be more pig—" catching herself she continues "—more resolute. It's my father, and family, and it is their business involved here; *you* have too much to lose Charles."

"Your father—The Peter Chardon Brooks, may have accumulated the largest fortune in Boston—"

"—which makes you the first rich Adams." She interrupts smiling.

"Ummm, at what cost?" Charles shook his head.

"Slaves are profitable." She said nonchalantly over her shoulder as they crossed the deck.

"Owning another human is morally wrong."

"Yes, but my family doesn't own them dear, we just ship them."

Dr. Hooker and three assistants arrived noisily at the Philadelphia jailhouse, clattering their wagon carts along the stone floor. The chests of 'scientific equipment': phrenic and phrenology charts and plaster casts of heads were the latest thing in science of the day.

As the doctor and his assistants unpacked, they watched the Africans, and the Africans watched them with some trepidation not knowing what all the instruments were as the doctors unpacked. Since captivity they had learned only minimal English. The doctor and assistants talked among themselves as though the Africans were not there. A fourth assistant entered cautiously—very nervous about being among the prisoners. He said nothing but watched everything.

The doctor unpacked a notebook and took out his new fountain pen which had just arrived from France. He unscrewed the cap and said, "You know, the one named Cinque, his countenance, for a native African, is unusually intelligent, evincing uncommon decision and coolness, with a composure characteristic of true courage."

The first assistant smiled, stared at the fountain pen, and asked "There's nothing to mark him as a malicious man?"

The second assistant "Ha. A fountain pen, I've heard of them, never seen one."

"Oh. By physiognomy and phrenology, the African, Cinque has considerable claim to benevolence."

The doctor wrote in his notebook, looked up and smiled at the assistant whose expression is a mirror of the Africans watching the doctor who kept talking and writing without dipping his pen in ink. "Hm. History says Ma'ād al-Mu'izz, the caliph of the Maghreb had a pen with an ink reservoir back in AD 973. But no one ever found it. So—eight hundred years later Schwenter made a pen with a reservoir. Maryland historian Hester Dorsey Richardson wrote a paper "About fountain pens from the 17th century" in 1827. I think he was Romanian, or maybe French—anyhow, inventor Petrache Poenaru got a patent from the French government for a fountain pen," He stopped writing and kept talking, switching subjects in mid-sentence. He pointed his pen at Cinque—then tapped the phrenology head. "According to Gall and Spurzheim, his moral sentiments and intellectual faculties predominate considerably over his animal propensities."

The jailhouse was an old stone building that smelled of chamber pots, old socks, and lye soap. The Marshal stood by the open door reading a newspaper to the jailer.

They all stopped by the cell door and waited for the jailer to find the proper key. Cinque leaned close to the iron bars to get a look at who was coming in. Dr. Hooker and his crew of four smiled at the Africans, unfolded two tables, and placed a variety of equipment and boxes on the tables. One assistant brought a bucket of water to mix with the plaster powder. Cinque watched them all place their equipment in some pre-arranged order. He was sure these were more instruments of power. He picked up a pair of calipers and smiled at the assistant, who was just being let into one of the cells by a marshal.

The line of curious men watched as the doctor and crew went about their "scientific" research. Acting as a tour guide, the jailer spoke as if he was a great expert on Africans. "That one, called Cinque, is said to have killed the captain and crew with his own hand, by cutting their throats."

"He expects to be executed?" the young assistant asked, cautiously taking the calipers from Cinque.

The doctor smiled, "Nevertheless, he manifests a sangfroid worthy of a stoic under similar circumstances."

The capitol lawn was cool and the morning mist was clearing off as Charles Francis Adams's coach clattered up the capitol's drive. Several army officers gathered by two targets on the lawn. Two hundred spectators and sixty congressmen stood to one side. Bunting and advertisements extolled the Colt repeat-action musket. John Quincy stood with several congressmen by a group of carriages. Charles walked to the Adams group. Benton, of Mississippi, stood apart with the Southern contingent. He held a prototype rifle and glared across the lawn at Adams.

Charles leaned to his father's ear as an officer reached for an Army musket, two others picked up the new repeating rifles. The two expert riflemen fired at targets, sighting, squeezing, and firing multiple times without reloading.

"Benton with a loaded weapon and you in sight is not healthy Father." "Humph, we have bulls at home with more dangerous tempers."

"Right now the most dangerous of all subjects disturbing the public temper is slavery—and *who* is in the forefront? My father. You and William Garrison."

"Disturbing the peace of the nation in the cause of justice."

"You know Garrison was hogtied and dragged through the streets of Boston. Boston, Father, and he had to be secretly put on a ship to England—just for writing about Amistad."

"I never liked Boston since they changed their name from Tremontaine."

"Well, the name Adams is a powder keg. I'm running for office father. What you're doing is killing me. The timing is bad. Just wait. Wait for a few months."

"The south is in a perpetual agony of trying to disguise itself behind bluster and pseudo-intellectual arguments...."

"Father —"

"Politicians court the South because they want their votes. Are you a politician? Politicians do not represent people. Politicians use politics to earn money at politics."

The first officer speedily reloaded as the other two continued—each with twelve shots in twelve seconds.

"Abolitionists are gathering themselves into bigger and bigger societies." "And their zeal's kindled a wildfire of passion against them."

"Father, the abolitionists are urging you to indiscreet actions."

"And, my own family exercise all the influence they possess to divert me from the abolitionists."

"It's politics—it's suicide Father. Despite all your violent opposition, the public in your own district is convulsed between slavery and abolition."

"And only they have the means to stop me."

"Calhoun over there doesn't look happy with you."

"Got an expression like someone choking a wet rooster."

"But you? Oh yes, lone warrior. Your badge of honor. Fight on."

"Ha, fight! I can run through the halls of Congress swinging a broad sword and not worry about slashing a friend."

"Well, despite your violent opposition, Texas will be added to the Union; father, vast new lands will be added to the nation. It is the era of Manifest Destiny."

"Isn't that wonderful! More slave states. Less Indian territory. A wild frontier backed by the capitalists of the East and applauded by the agrarians of the South."

"Railroads are striking West. The telegraph. It's a modern world Father. Money is the new aristocracy. We are a nation of over ten million. New York with seven hundred thousand is one of the great cities of the world."

"So. The mob has taken power."

The three young Adams aides bantered good naturedly back and forth as they angled through the crowd, walked around horses and past several noisy platoons of soldiers and weapon wagons, to join Adams who watched the firearms display closely.

"Adams has a full plate, how can he take it all on James?

"Well, he doesn't drink 'til midnight does he?"

"Then only applejack."

"Unlike the rest of congress," James laughed.

"Every congressman in the pub would love to scalp him."

"You make enemies here just bringin' him a glass of water, for God's sake."

"Ha. Learn to dodge faster." James ducked around a team of matched Clydesdales. The three jump back as a volley of fire startled a team of horses. Two soldiers are quick to grab their reins and quiet them.

"Well, for the last thousand years he's insulted the most powerful people in the world. Seems to thrive on it."

"Ha. Old news. Why shouldn't he stick his nose in the Amistad mess?" James halted as two cavalrymen mount their horses.

"Old? News is it you want? You've missed the papers for the last five minutes? Let me see... How about the Briggs Cotton Co. losing millions in New Orleans. Failed! Oh, and panic in every bank east of the Mississippi."

"In New York, banks are freezing accounts. Banks in Boston, Philadelphia and Baltimore closed. An extra session of Congress is being called."

"Oh, and that little incident," Lynn countered.

"The Patriot war! America and Canada?" William finished Lynn's thought.

"Oh, oh, even better. General Thomas Sidney Jesup—he's the one who called it the Seminole war—'The Negro War' to scare up the southern slavers, though the Indians did own some slaves—anyhow, besides leading the longest most expensive Indian war, he arbitrarily imprisons all the Seminole chiefs and started a war in Florida," Lynn smirked.

"The Steamer Caroline was burned—by Canadians." William added again.

"Let's see... and Atherton from New Hampshire introduced a gag resolution preventing discussion of slavery on the house floor. That's really aimed just for Mr. Adams."

"Well, that did piss the ol' man off," James nodded.

"Oh, President—Van Buren? of the United States? His State message says anti-slavery documents should not be allowed in the US mail," Lynn added.

"That was a piss off too," William laughed.

"Now. Did I forget anything?!"

"Oh, really? The Graves of Kentucky and Cilley of New Hampshire duel?" James looked heavenward.

Lynn sarcastically waved William off with a laugh. "Ha. Rules of the house don't cover *gentlemen* of the house; shooting at each other—well, till Cilley got killed!"

"Ironically by a congressman named Graves." James smirked.

"Oh, but that goes on all the time."

James stopped. "Ha. Look you two, Mr. Adams didn't go looking for a duel. He's a constitutionalist."

The three aides almost sighed at once, "The government isn't divided enough?"

"Well, it's sure a test for voters."

All three nod at the unhappy, departing, Charles Adams.

"Charles Franci is still at the ol' man."

James shook his head, "And Charles's wife, and his father-in-law."

"He looks a bit peaked," Lynn said.

"A bit peaked? Ha, pecked is more like it!"

"Besides, Charles is running for the House of Representatives, Adams ain't helpin' his chances," William warned.

"Interesting," Lynn nodded.

"Oh, and may you live in interesting times." James laughed.

Senator Baldwin and an aide spotted Adams and approached as a blast of gunfire echoed around the buildings. His three young aides presented serious faces to Adams. James handed John Quincy Adams a folder. Baldwin and his aide nodded at the four and waited for Quincy to acknowledge them.

"Sir, on the 4th of September Lewis Tappan did appeal to the Friends of Humanity for donations to help the Africans," James glanced at Baldwin as he said it.

Balwin, smiled, and added, "It was in the Emancipator."

"The Circuit Judge decided the United States doesn't exercise the right..." Baldwin interrupted, "Of all other *civilized* nations..."

The aide quickly added, "...to prosecute piracy on foreign ships."

The second aide interjected, "Therefore, he cannot try them for piracy or murder." Baldwin continued "But they can try the Africans to determine if they're slaves or not."

"Will it be tried in Connecticut or Washington?" Adams asked.

"No one knows yet," Baldwin's assistant added.

"What about the Africans?" Adams opened the envelope, scanned the three pages quickly.

"They'll be held as slaves," an aide says as the volley of firing stops and new rifles are handed to the riflemen. Adams's shoulders tensed as much at that news as the new volley erupting in back of their group.

"Mr. Baldwin, you have a mean way with words. Construct a note, and one of you take it to the Secretary of Navy. That: Congress in general and myself in particular would look upon the Navy budget, now before us, with a very grave and unfriendly eye if anything calamitous befell the Africans while under the Navy's protection."

More gunshots. Several nervous horses bolted and half a dozen enlisted men chased after them. Distracted, Baldwin shook his head. "You would think after all their training they had those horses wouldn't be skittish around violence."

"You could say the same about Congress," Adams quipped.

Smiling, Baldwin and his aide walked away quickly. The audience applauded as two privates ran across the lawn, took down the targets, and held them up for the group to see, showing all the bulls-eyes.

Green and Fordham's lawyer filed against Gedney and Meade, stating Green and Fordham had rescued the cargo of the ship by capturing the Africans on the beach. Ruiz and Montez sued, saying the slaves were their property. The Spanish government argued that, since the *Amistad* was taken by a U.S. Navy armed ship, the United States, under international treaty, had to return the ship and its cargo to the Spanish owners. An attorney for the United States government appeared before the court and presented this request. This attorney also argued that, if the Africans could not legally be returned to Ruiz and Montez, the court should order them sent back to Africa. The African's team of lawyers responded by asserting—since they were free men in Africa, who had been kidnapped and sold to the Spanish slave traders, who traded illegally, they should be released from custody and set free.

CHAPTER SEVEN

Library of Congress

Adams and James waited in his coach as two young aides scurried down the library steps carrying loads of legal books to his carriage. Every book was full of yellow paper page strips sticking out like porcupine quills. The aides also piled books and file folders from Adam's office on the seat, and floor, then they tried to find space for themselves. Adams sorted through a stack of correspondence and handed a fistful to each of the battered and bruised, but smiling, young aides. John Quincy Adams read as the carriage bumped along the streets of Washington DC.

"Hear, read these out loud while I look for something," Adams barked.

"Ah, sir, some of these letters are—personal," James said hesitantly.

"I know what they are. I don't know what they say. Now, if we are to be assiduous, and since you are doing nothing, and I have to look for something, efficiency demands you do something. Hm? You shall be my ravens."

"Sir?" William looks up.

"Remember, 1 Kings 17-6 Elijah is fed by a flock of ravens."

"Ravens?" James shrugged.

"They weren't kosher, being scavengers, but they saved Elijah," Adams points at the stack of papers in James lap.

"Oh."

James leaned to the window using the last rays of sunlight to read by. "A letter from Miss. Pierce, East Marlborough, in a good hand, if flowery and full of enthusiasm, shows good composition indicating a cultivated mind and liberal education, full of flattery."

"We are not grading them James, these are constituents! What does she want!?"

"Yes sir. Ah, she seems to be an abolitionist and would like a reproduction of your defense oratory." He puts down that letter in a starting a pile.

"Next?" The other aide immediately starts reading.

"An invitation from the citizens of Springfield to a public dinner, on the third, for the opening of the railroad from Boston."

"You would think we could use stamps like the Brits, the Penny Black and Two Penny Blue."

"You'd just have to lick the stamps, and still have to open an envelope to get to what you don't even want to read," James sighed.

"Next?" Adams grumbled.

James started right up. "An Appeal from the Friends of Humanity for donations."

"Next!" Adams continues to shuffle through stacks of papers and pages without looking up.

"An invitation from the Massachusetts Charitable Mechanic Association. He says that the Amistad trial should never have been interfered with by Van Buren."

The coach rattled over cobblestones causing correspondence to flutter about as young aides, who many laughingly called Adams's body guards, grabbed at letters trying to keep the loose papers in the coach. Adams looked up amused, then dived back into the stack in front of him.

"Next."

"A note from Congressman Preston thanking you for your support against Calhoun and the land giveaway."

"Hmm."

"Rives of Virginia assailing you for not supporting his right to his seat."

"Thompson wants to talk to you privately about your damn isolationist protectionist Silk Bill. Ahh, his words sir."

"My what!" Adams looks up and growls at the wrong young man.

"I didn't say that," Lynn recoiled. "It's what he says…"

William holds up the letter. "Ah, sir, Spain rejects all claims, and insists everything be returned to Spain."

"Everything! Damnation, they're human beings not things James! Next!"

"Ingersoll's reply to you about the five-million Treasury Note," Lynn said carefully. Adams waved his hand as if chasing flies. "Next."

"Department of State, Chief Clerk, Martin with a discussion about the letter from Holabird, the United States District Attorney of Connecticut of 21st of September, states that: It's jurisdiction–"

"JESUS CHRIST!" Adams glares at James.

"Sorry sir. The word 'no' had been removed from the original letter from the manuscript copy transmitted to the House. It should read the United States Circuit Court had decided that it had NO jurisdiction…"

"Ah ha! Hold that out."

"No name. Ah. Well…" William pauses.

"What?!"

"Well…" William stops.

"Well, well!?" John Quincy Adams grumbles.

"It's some suggestion about cutting off your private parts… sir," William blurts out. "Ha, the man obviously doesn't know anything about politics, we have nothing private. I'll take that letter. Well, only one castration threat, no major decapitation or bizarre execution threats, I must be slipping." He pulls out his pocket watch, clicks it open and smiles.

"Slipping?"

"You've heard me debase John Henry Eaton? An indecent man, a licentious life—he and others have made themselves my adversaries, solely for their own advancement, and have forfeited the characters of gentlemen, to indulge the bitterness of their self-stirred gall. Thomas Hart Benton has the principles of a highway robber, Martin Van Buren those of a dirty intriguer, and John C. Calhoun's actions were mere prostitution to popularity." Adams looks out the window. "Ah, we've made good time, only seven-twenty. Now if you gentlemen would be so kind as to unload this confusion; the day is still young, maybe we can get some work done."

John Adams stepped out of the coach and looked up to the black driver. "Thank you, Jeremy. You can pick me up tomorrow morning at five."

Ye Old Stone Inn was not the average DC bar, it was in a modernly expensive inn. The low murmur and occasional outburst of laughter cut through the heavy cigar and pipe smoked bar. Bar room cigar smoke became universal after 1762 when mister Putnam returned home from England's Cuban war to Hartford. He brought back

30,000 Cuban cigars and a bag full of seeds that started an industry in Connecticut. In this particular barroom, smoke and hubbub covered the conversation in a far corner table. Benton and five men argued, Benton was nervous, his mouth formed every word cautiously. He did not really want to be seen with these men, but their constituents were traders with money, by his standards they were low class, even crass. Their words overlapped, rose and fell as they drank beer and shots, two pitchers and a bottle in front of them had been well used. It's hard to tell who said what because they tended to try to finish each other's sentences and the crowded room was loud. A concertina and fiddle started up, adding rhythm to the laugher from the bar, the street noises, and the door banging open and close punctuated their diatribe.

"Don't profane the word congressman with damned Adams' name God Dammit!"

"Yeah, somethin's gotta to be done about th' bastard." "Shhhhh," Benton's head jerks around nervously.

"No! It's a free country. I say what the hell I want. Where the hell I want." "There's just no shutting th' fucker up!"

"An ounce of lead is the cure!"

"Well, if that idiot Dr. Tolson had any balls he'd a shot damned Adams."

"Damn foreigner—caught stealin' from the army, deserved to be fired, doctor or no," Benton quipped.

"Ha, damned Adams fired him." Clifton turned looking for a barmaid.

"Ha. Tolson shoulda fired back," Lanier snorted.

"I ain't funnin', damn it. You remember the Louisiana hangin'? Berserk nigras hung a white—five hundred of 'em got to rampagin'."

"Yes, yes, and five hundred o' them was kicked the hell out a by the militia."

"An US troops."

"It only took a couple a weeks."

"Couple—hell a dozen plantations was sacked."

"Old news."

Clifton kept waving at the barmaid. No response. He stood, grumbling. "Okay, this one's on me," and weaves his way to the bar.

"Abolitionist just drooling over it happening' again."

Benton was quick to say, "Adams says he's not an abolitionist, but he's the damned scourge of the Southern block."

"He's the major trouble to the slaveocracy in Congress."

"He gets nourishment from the rage he stirs up in slave states."

"Tell me somefin I don't know."

"And, the addlepated Yankee press parrots his every profanity."

"There's 'nough who'd quiet him."

"I once put a bullet in Jackson but—not damned Adams—he's in congress," Benton growls.

Lanear sat next to Benton nodding, he smirked, "There's things worse than death could happen."

"Damn Adams anyhow. Lanear's right."

"Anti-Christ Anarchist."

"And them heathen Amistad niggrahs gonta' cause a uprising. A cataclysm." A noisy new group invades the bar and the the music gets even louder. "Beulah-land's gonna explode," Lanear almost has to shout. "He's the devil's aide."

"He has to be stopped."

"Stopped yes. Not permanently." Benton's fist hit the table hard. Surprised at himself, he looked around quickly to see if anyone noticed his anger. But the room was way too loud to bother.

"Just shoot him," Lanear glared, leaned back with arms out—like 'what's the problem.'

Clifton shuffles back to the table with a fresh pitcher of ale.

"God-damned Lawrence drew down on Jackson with two guns and Old fuckin' Hickory beat him up with his cane."

"That idiot prosecuting attorney Key couldn't shut him up."

"Lawrence ranted forever at ever-one in the court."

"Ha. Refused to recognize the legitimacy of the court."

"Unfortunately, damned Adams ain't Francis Scott Key."

"Damn his bones."

"He's a lunatic!"

"I heard they gonna kidnap the Niggrahs and take them to Canada."

"Hidin' them under a train I heard."

"I'm telling you they only—" Lanear made a cutting motion across his throat.

"Damn it, he's a member of the Congress," Benton exhaled.

Lenear looks at Benton surprised. "So?"

"Good! Between the eyes."

"Once you take that road there's no return. A duel's one thing. I'll not back assassins. There's no honor there."

"There's no returnin' now."

"Fuck honor, we talking slavery or abolition."

"Wake up. The government's getting too big. I keep sayin' it—too big. It's destroying our rights and he's kindling to the fire that'll burn us all."

"States rights. It's God's work!"

"It is my duty to leave nothing undone that I may lawfully do, to pull down this administration."

"And none too soon. He's a insult to God's creation."

"They who with their eyes open, persist in hugging the traitor to their bosom, deserve to be insulted...deserve to be slaves, with no other music to soothe them but the clank of the chains which they have put on themselves and given to their offspring," Benton said and took a long draft of beer.

"Part of one a your speechifies?" Baker smirked and shook his head. "Ha. You and abolitionist John Randolph with his four hundred slaves."

"They're eatin' away the constitution."

"We all know what it means."

"The South has to protect itself."

Lanear leaned in closer. "Well, the solution is—no trial."

"Ha! Well thank you Mr. Genius," Baker almost spewed his beer.

"No! No trial, no problems. No Adams. No Nigrahs—no trial." Lanear puts his fist up to Baker's face and started to count on his fingers.

"First. You are the dumbest SOB—..."

"No, no, it's just a little matter of kidnapping the nigrahs."

"Come on?! That's the dumbest...Well, how? Rope's easier," Baker growls.

"We just get us some good ol' boys..."

"An some rope..."

"No. I'll go along with the kidnapping, Lanear, but we give them back to the Spanish. No killing."

"Fuckin' spoil sport."

In the dark of night, by the river, on the loading docks, the faded name Louis Tappan painted in large letters was just readable on the large three-story brick warehouse. Several painted illustrations of dry goods filled the rest of the brick wall. A shadow of a figure ran around the corner and pounded on the metal double doors. A door opened. Butts slipped in quickly. Tappan looked both ways, slammed the door and bolted it behind them. Butts was out of breath.

"Butts. What is it?"

"The President ordered the man o' war Grampus to New Haven."

"New Haven?! But they're in New London. Does Baldwin, or Adams know?

Still breathing hard Butts gasped, "It's top secret. The Federal court In New Haven? They'll go by coach to the docks, then the ships'll stand by to take the prisoners to be tried in Havana."

"How?!"

"I don't know. I just heard. Chappel was at the Bird and Bottle, and Meade was there with his cronies drinking. Lieutenant Meade let slip that he was going to Havana to testify against Cinque. So…"

"But they're taking them from New Haven to Hartford jail."

"It'll take the Grampus four days to get here from Washington."

"Judas Priest!"

"I was hoping we could do this in the courts here."

"I'll get word to Tubman, and Coffin."

"Dutch's organized almost a hundred men to kidnap the blacks and go through the underground railroad to get them to Canada."

In Washington DC it was politically expedient to be seen at the concerts; despite the economic depression, concerts were regularly booked and attended. While the average worker earned five hundred dollars a year, Wilson and Shirreff did well for themselves, Mrs. Shirreff earning over thirty-eight thousand dollars in 1840 and that was after expenses. Their itinerary was a mixture of Italian operatic arias, some Scottish ballads, and French opera. They waited behind the curtain while the orchestra organized their notes, tuned their instruments, then turned one to the other as they gossiped before a concert.

The first violin whispered hoarsely. "Cinque and the others were taken to New London."

The bass player ran his thumb over the horsehairs on his bow and nodded, "And indicted for murder and piracy."

The flute player turned in his chair as he listened, "That Cuban, Montez, claimed them as his property."

Woodwind closed his case and looked up, "Look, the murder is the thing. Everyone gets sidetracked. It was bloody murder."

The French horn player shook his head, "The two captains filed salvage claims for the Amistad."

"Have you seen what some of the Boston newspapers been writing?"

"How they can be called newspapers is beyond me."

"A ferocious disregard of decency."

"There was the story of cannibals eating the crew."

"Good God Henry, you don't really believe that."

"Twas in the paper."

"They put any claptrap in that paper anyone can make up."

"Maybe there're people who would like you to believe that."

"Me?"

"Everyone Henry. Maybe it's because they want slavery not justice."

"Well, they never found the crew did they?"

"Henry? They must have thrown them overboard."

Second woodwind's eyes followed the notes on his music stand, "They're murderers! The slave thing's just a defense trick to divert you from the murders."

The third brass player in line added, "Well, the officers of the US Washington also filed claims."

"They said because of the anti-slave treaty of 1820 that it's illegal for any nation of the Western hemisphere to import slaves," The second violin tuned his instrument.

The trombone player smiled, "So any child born after the treaty Is supposed to be set free. So let the kids go. But the others…"

"It doesn't matter if they were slaves or not; they murdered the crew," The trombone player added.

"There wouldn't been a murder if they weren't taken as slaves." The second trombone huffed.

The woodwind player looked to heaven and went, "Tsk. Tsk!"

The oboe player walked past the group to his chair, "High priced lawyers. Bah! You think you or I could afford one of them let alone four, and one an ex-president!?"

Timpani tapped his foot to some tune, "It's the Queen of Spain."

Woodwind laughed, "Oh come on, she's a twelve-year-old."

"Ha," the trombone player laughed, "And smarter than all the lawyers in Philadelphia."

"Paper said she and her ministers forged the deeds and concealments in Cuba to get around the law. It's money in her pocket."

Click, click, click. The conductor was at the podium. All but two turn and play Mozart.

"Of course! Wouldn't you? Little girl got five dollars a head."

"Let's see—more than two hundred and fifty thousand slaves since the treaty times five.—Even you could live on that. Might keep her in shoes."

"Now I hear Adams has petitioned the President's papers! The president, can you imagine!?"

Shirreff and Wilson walked on stage—applause. The conductor raised his baton, glared at the woodwind player. The orchestra started.

CHAPTER EIGHT

New London Pub

Loud music, full house, hearsay, rumor, and scuttlebutt. Ever since the Amistad was brought to bay the town was full of gossip. Some gossip more interesting than others—some unnerving.

Barnaby leaned close to the bartender and whispered not too discreetly. "I'm tellin' you that's scouts. Scouts!"

"What?" The bartender twisted the beer keg tap closed and looked up annoyed that the adjective, predicate, verb, and whatever is missing from this conversation.

"Who?" he asked, irritated.

"Scouts."

"Scouts? What?"

"Scouts! Like Indians?!" Another barfly put his hand up, covering his mouth as if he really didn't want anyone else to know the importance of his secret information.

"Na you twit. Not scouts. They're part of the African navy." Barnaby, the longshoreman who was almost sitting in the barfly's lap, smirked.

"African Navy. Are you —" That was a surprise but—sounded real enough—so he tapped the top of his mug and ordered another.

"Yes! The Nigger Navy I tell you!"

"You been sucking' laudanum again?" the barman laughed.

"S'true all along the Barbary coast Frogs and Limeys 're arming them ta get back at us."

"Now they's comin' over here?" Barney slurped his beer.

"It's true. They's a black fleet just patrollin', off the coast jus' waiting."

"They come ashore to grab some white meat. Oh, yes," Barnaby burped. "They eat us."

"Jesus."

"You crazy!"

"It's true." Barnaby tried to find the bar with his elbow. Missed.

"Grab us, our women, for slaves."

"And sell us in Africa?" Barnaby tapped his empty glass top. "White slaves in Africa!!?"

The barkeep put down four more beers and a brandy.

"And our women, they particular got to have white women. Yes."

"Ship loads of them waitin' just over the horizon."

"We can't let 'em get away."

"Now they know our towns, our roads."

"They like ants. Black ants! They go back an tell all them othern, and you know, first thing, there gonna be a black army right here. Yes," Barnaby burped loudly, focused unsteadily on his beer, and dropped his shot glass in his nearly full mug.

The 1824 fraud. The big scandal of the day, to add to all the rest within the year, was that Henry Clay, the new speaker of the House of Representatives, held a deciding position. In the 1824 presidential election Clay finished fourth with 37 electoral college votes. Andrew Jackson pulled 99 and won the popular vote by 48,149 votes, J Q Adams had 84 electoral and 113,122 popular votes—until Clay threw his votes to Adams. Clay ran mean attacks against Jackson, a man he detested. Clay was accused so bitterly by the opposition that he forged a coalition to secure the White House for John Quincy Adams. Adams named Clay as his Secretary of State, a stepping-stone to the presidency next time. This backfired on Adams and Clay. The Jackson press yelled "corrupt payoff" the even nastier, maybe the nastiest, presidential race ever, was 1828. It began even as Adams took office with all the accusations of fake election, and fraud in America.

Then, just three years later Jackson decided to dismantle the Bank of the United States and was censured by Congress for refusing to turn over documents. The Senate passed legislation to renew the bank's charter and Jackson vetoed it. Congress overruled Jackson's veto. Jackson swore he wanted to shoot Clay. Wiser heads said, "No, no! Kentuckian Clay was a superb shot."

"I Don't want to duel him damnit, I just want to shoot him," Jackson growled. This from a man who had survived numerous duels.

Just to complicate matters Spain was slowly losing its grip on territory around the world. Before Great Britain outlawed the slavery that Spain controlled in Cuba, the Philippines, Puerto Rico and Guam, Spain claimed 60 percent of continental North America, and 70 percent of South America and it was getting paid a tax on every slave sent from Spanish territory—legally or not.

Spain demanded the release of the Amistad, the return of the slaves and Mendes, and Ruiz to Spain. The British government, not to be left out of a good international argument demanded that the treaty against trading in slaves be upheld and the offenders arrested.

Isabella the first became the Spanish queen on the death of her husband; Isabella II was three years old in 1833 when JQ Adams negotiated the transfer of Florida from Spain to America. Soon after that the king of Spain bent the rules of Salic Law, which decreed that succession of the throne go to the direct male line. Salian, (a dynasty of the High Middle Ages) Franks, and Germanic tribes, followed the law of excluding women from inheriting land. Problem was, King Ferdinand VII of Spain fathered two daughters, Isabella and Luisa. So, he decreed that his daughter, rather than his brother, would succeed him. Ferdinand's brother, Don Carlos, was not happy. This led to the First Carlist War, 1833-1839, Isabella I's mother, and General Espartero, were regents for Isabella II. A complicated round of international bidding to marry Isabella II started between the royalty of France, Spain, and Britain. This all helped lead to the French uprisings and to Louis-Philippe's defeat. Isabella was eleven at the Amistad trials end.

The Van Buren administration was sympathetic with the Spanish demands, but Secretary of State Forsyth opined that the president could not release the *Amistad,* the slaves, or Mendes, and Ruiz, because American law states the president cannot interfere with the judiciary— besides the Spanish traders were then in the state of Connecticut's jurisdiction.

The court, undeterred by the president, ruled the Africans had acted as free men, they had to fight to escape their kidnapping and illegal confinement. Van Buren was under tremendous pressure particularly from the Southern states, to order the case sent to the Supreme Court. On March 9, 1840; the Supreme Court agreed with the lower court ruling authorizing the release of the Africans and their return to Africa.

Umbral forms, emerging from the dusky mist, and as quiet as a group of twenty-five men on horseback could be, they made their way from the west to New London docks through the outskirts of town in the near morning light. No one else was on the street. They dismounted by a small park and tethered their horses behind the heavy shrubbery. Several of the men were from the New London pub meeting with Walker, many were slave owners. They quietly crept behind a hedge that ran along the street. Lanear carried a roll of rope over his shoulder. Another dozen of the group hurried across the street, split up and hid in an alley behind a plank fence that ran next to the buildings. A second group arrived from the east, unbeknownst to the first group only three blocks away.

One of the men, Dutch, quietly entered the church with a rifle and made his way to the stairs and up a ladder to the bell tower. Another ten men assembled behind the church. The rest of the group of twenty positioned themselves along the side of a stone building at a crossroads. The first bird calls of morning started. Dutch grumbled, watching one of the men run across the road. He motioned several more to get down, then waited, watching the crossroads intently.

A hoot came from the church tower. They all looked up—hoof beats and the clatter of wagon wheels; the group grabbed their rifles. Dutch, in the church tower, drew a bead on where the wagons would appear around the corner.

At the crossroads, looming like giants, two huge open wagons of Marines in uniform sat back-to-back in two rows with rifles at the ready. Four coaches with the Africans followed. Each of the coaches had two Marines sitting on top. They were followed by two more wagons full of Marines. The glow of sun warmed the hazy morning and glistened off fifty Marines's weapons. Wide eyed, Dutch saw the Marines, and they were alert, looking for trouble, rifles at the ready. Ducking fast, Dutch pulled his rifle down, clanging the bell. Two men thought that a signal and started into the middle of the road. They saw the wagon bristling with Marines and ran back. The men behind the stone building dived out of sight. The convoy rushed on. Three blocks later, a dozen men stood in the middle of the road, recognized the bright uniforms of the Marine-loaded wagons, and scattered back behind the hedge with the rest of the gang as the caravan clattered by.

April 29th, 1840

Three judges ate lunch in New Haven court chambers. Judge Thompson stood at the window and watched a black tar and rag dummy dragged across the lawn and strung up from a tree in front of the courthouse by five men. A passerby stopped to argue with the men who threw a rope over an old maple tree limb. One of the lynchers, Lanear, shouted back at the passerby, two others stomped over and started pushing—that started a brawl. Two men unloading a wagon joined in the shoving match. Two armed officers from the courthouse jogged over and yelled at the lynchers who ran across the street dodging horses and carriages, and several women who hurried out of the way.

Judge Thompson sighed and turned from the window to face the others. "The point is a perplexing one, and if I decide against it—an appeal could be carried to the Supreme Court..."

The second judge nodded, "And in case the decision were reversed?"

The third judge added, "The case would come back for a hearing on the main question..."

"And would be appealed again," the second judge smiled, shook his head and poured a healthy shot of Bourbon into a cut crystal Masonic whisky glass.

Thompson pointed at the bottle and the second judge handed him a glass, he poured deeply, held his glass up to the light of the window, "Ah, thank the lord, President Washington sent 13,000 armed militia into Pennsylvania to collect whisky taxes or we wouldn't –"

"Be needlessly delayed," Judge Thompson interrupted "Therefore, as the case would be appealed, I choose to affirm the decision for Judge Judson pro-forma, and leave the whole case to be decided by the Supreme Court, which sits at Washington in January."

"So, September 19th, 1839 in Hartford, Justice Thompson ruled the court had no jurisdiction since the crimes were at open sea on a Spanish vessel. And as for the claims of the salvage, they would have to be taken up in the United States District Court where the ship was captured."

"Well, if that ain't a beautiful side step and do-si-do," the second judge huffed.

In the White House reading room Van Buren slammed a newspaper down on the desk. Four others in the room were startled by the violence as he growled,

"Damned Adams and the court anyhow. Look at this, this, this ruling!"

"Adams and Tappan are obviously afraid we'll try to get the Africans out of the court's jurisdiction." Ingersoll eased out of the couch, clipped the end off a Punch cigar, looked at Van Buren who waved him to go ahead, light it. "So he had Attorney General Sedgwick file charges of kidnapping."

"Kidnapping!" Ban Buren barked in disbelief.

"Kidnapping, false imprisonment, and assault," the second aide mumbled as he read from pages at hand.

"Against Montez and Ruiz?! Jesus! What kind of world do we live in? Lawyers! Just to tie up and complicate the case." Van Buren huffed and sat behind his huge desk.

"The Spanish Ambassador is furious, of course!" Ingersoll sighed.

"Well, they immediately raised bail." Added an aide.

"But Ruiz and Montez seem awfully sure of southern sympathy."

"They think Adams is a senile old man," Van Buren said glaring into his empty glass.

Ingersoll added quickly, "More fool they. They think they're going to make martyrs of themselves, so they happily declined bail." He waved his right hand in the air like an escaping bird.

"Well, I say their thinking's faulty," Van Buren growled.

"That damned old man is up at five workin' fourteen hours a day," added Ingersoll. "Nothin' to color his opinions except a congressional salary." Ingersoll looked up at Van Buren who was trying to juggle a stuck cut glass top of a whisky container and pour another healthy slug.

"Waddy Thompson had the right idea—they should have censored God damned Adams. Extending rights to slaves? Rights belonging only to free men! That's—that's inciting slaves to insurrection."

"Well hell that was then—this is now."

"Ah damnit! But he's the only man I know who squelched Daniel Webster."

"Worse yet, he's a bloody puritan." Ingersoll laughed.

"Meanwhile, Montez and Ruiz 'r in jail. Argh." Van Buren made a face and put his feet up on an ottoman and sighed, cursing his gout.

Ingersoll droned on, "The British ministers demanded the laws of Spain against the slave trade be enforced against Don Jose Ruiz and Don Pedro Montez for buying Negroes they knew were recently imported illegally from Africa."

"Well, that ought to make our two Spanish friends overjoyed; because it looks like they may be martyrs for quite a while. Get to Judson and rub some salt in his hide."

"Hell you jus don't know which way Judson's gonna jump."

"Judson may be a U.S. representative from Connecticut and a district judge for Connecticut and served in their House of Representatives, and a member of the Toleration Party, and in the American Colonization Society, but —"

"He advocates sending Africans back to Africa."

"But will he want them to be sent back to Africa… or Spain?"

"That dog jus' don't hunt."

The president held the bourbon container up and sadly squinted at what was left in the bottom.

While Ruiz and Montez were marched into New York jail and put into a cell—Judge Judson sat in his chambers stung by presidential barbs, constitutional assault, and agitated by a pile of threatening letters on his desk. He read one with a presidential seal—wadded it, and angrily threw it across the room.

A group of eight men sat in Tappan's warehouse in New York on boxes, barrels and stacks of sacks that circled Tappan, who paced as he talked, "I'm convinced that president Van Buren wants this case dismissed quickly with as little publicity as possible."

Dr. Gibbs looked around at the group as he started, "The President needs the support of the South to stay in office. He'd be on that side of the fence anyhow. He's pro-slaver, he's always been a pro-slaver an' he ain't changing."

"Louis, they're thinking: if this Black revolt goes unpunished, what'll be the effect on a couple of million slaves in the South?"

"They're couple million slaves too late to think that." Gibbs added.

"Before we can defend them we have to communicate with them. We have to understand the Africans's language."

Tappan agreed. "Well, I have a team of young Yale language majors."

"We need a real translator." Gibbs added sarcastically. "Hebrew, Greek and Latin don't seem to have any roots in the African language."

"Yes, yes, what we need is an African who speaks English. Know any?"

"Well, there's lots of them."

Exasperated Gibbs added, "But they just don't happen to speak Mende."

"Mende?"

"Yes, Lord there're about four hundred different languages in Africa."

"What about Antonio?"

"Antonio's vocabulary is very limited. Besides, he belonged to the dead captain. He's held as property of the estate until this is all sorted out."

Gibbs held up five coins. Phillips smiled, "What's this? You buying?"

Gibbs smirked, shook his head, "That's a five dollar gold piece."

"One?"

Gibbs smile broadens, "Yes. Now, how many?"

Phillips goes along with Gibbs game, "That's ten, fifteen, twenty, twenty-five."

"No," Gibbs corrects, "two, three, four, and five."

Phillips insists, "No, no, it's ten, fifteen, twenty, and a five an that's twenty-five dollars."

"It's five coins. Alright. What's that?"

"Ah, I said twenty-five dollars."

"Not the amount, the number," Gibbs sighed.

"Don't get uppity; three times ten is thirty, that's the number."

"No—The number of coins!?"

"Ah, well, why didn't you say so."

"Because no one speaks your language."

Butts added with a laugh, "Well, I hope to God you find an African smarter than Phillips."

"No. We just ask the Africans to count Mende. 1,2,3,4,5. Then we tour the docks and markets of New Haven, Boston, and New York, repeating the Mende numbers until we find our man."

CHAPTER NINE

The New York docks were a forest of masts and a jumble of free blacks hauling goods from ships and to ships. Several of Phillip's and Gibb's young men made their way through the maze of dock activity as they followed Dr. Gibbs. Going from African to African along the bustling docks they asked if they spoke Mende.

Stevedores, teamsters, crews and passengers, crowded around wagons, carriages, luggage, and produce. The team stopped to ask two black men unloading luggage from a carriage. One smiled and wiped his brow. Pointed at the next dock. "Mende man? No, no. Not here. All Ghana man here. Maybe on next dock."

September 14th, 1839

It was a quiet scene seen through the soot-stained window of the Pennsylvania Freeman Press glowing with orange lamplight, a print room typesetter and a young assistant printer's devil worked with unbelievable speed picking type out of a bin and arranging columns in a wooden box. In the background two presses were being cleaned. Whittier read copy out to the typesetter as two other men stacked paper being readied for press, and an artist finished carving a wood block of the Africans.

The typesetter read the last bit of set type, "All the Africans, with the exception of Burna, B.u.r.n.a. who was sick, were taken to Hartford to await trial. The libels and claims in relation to the Amistad were read and filed as follows... Next?" He looked up at the waiting Whittier.

Whittier continued, "One. Lt. G.e.d.n.e.y and M.e.a.d.e, filed their libel praying for salvage. Two. Captain Green, of Long Island put in his libel for salvage. Three. Pedro M.o.n.t.e.z filed his libel against part of the cargo and four slaves. Four. J.o.s.e. R.u.i.z. filed libel against the remainder of the slaves and property. Read that first bit back."

The typesetter read as the boy and Whittier watched and listened.

"Lastly: Mr. B.r.a.i.n.a.r.d. opened the argument on behalf of the libelists, Lt. Gedney and Meade. He contended that whether the Africans were or were not property of Ruiz, the Court could not set them free; crime had been committed on board the Spanish vessel, and this government was bound to deliver up these persons to Spain. Regardless his clients had performed meritorious services, for which they were justly entitled to salvage... They should hang the bloody..."

Whittier glared at the typesetter, "Don't editorialize, just set what I wrote."

"The National Journal..." The typesetter started to add.

"Henry, the partisan editors at the National Journal and their ilk print any damned poison to advance their cause and circulation. It's News Fiction. Scandal sells. You should know that by now."

"People 'r believein' it."

"Say any fool thing enough and lots a folks will." Whittier exhaled.

Henry added, "The Southern states passed laws against any publications writing good about abolitionism, there just ain't freedom of the press on anything dealing with slavery. It's a question that jus' doesn't exist in Southern states."

Whittier nodded.

"Well hell, they got the Congress all tied up in arcane writs that table anything—what the hell's law for anyhow?"

Outside, a gathering mob in the dark street pried loose pavement stones on their march to Whittier's paper. *Crash!* The words "Pennsylvania Freeman" on the glass window shattered. The mob surged in. The apprentice and carver were knocked unconscious. The mob beat Whittier, dumped ink, scattered type, broke a press. Fire broke out and the mob ran out shouting racist slurs as Whittier and the typesetter staggered up, grabbed the printer's devil, two helpers, and staggered to the back door.

October 23rd, 1839

It's a four holer outhouse but only one other person was sitting on the far hole. So James sat, rattled the paper, snapped it open, and folded it in half to the page he was reading. He looked past the pile of dried corncobs and old handbills at the student reading a math book and rattled the paper again and read out loud from the New York Herold:

"The extraordinary arrest and imprisonment of Messer's Ruiz and Montez, at the suit of the Amistad savages, instigated by the abolitionists, will come up today before Judge Ingle is for further review and examination. It is expected, therefore that some strange and curious development will be made relative to the conduct of intrigues of the abolitionists, the arrogant interference of Lewis Tappan, and the uses to which these savages have been put by the fanatics.

"This matter, in connection with the abolition intrigues, is beginning to assume the most revolting and audacious character—a character that makes the blood boil and the heart burn. On the arrival of the savages in this country, with their hands crimsoned with the blood of white men, they were seized upon by a band of fanatics, who, under the banner of humanity and religion, have been levying contributions on the public while they were proposing to teach the slaves the elements of religion and civilization."

"My . God . He does go on, and on!" James grumbled and went on.

"They knew nothing of our constitution, laws or language of the country upon which they were thus thrown and accused as pirates and murderers. Claimed as slaves of the very men who were their captives, they were deprived even of the faculty of speech in their own defense. This condition was sorely calamitous; it claimed from the humanity of a civilized nation compassion; it claimed from the brotherly love of a Christian land sympathy; it claimed from a republic professing reverence for the rights of man , justice, and what have we done?

"A naval officer of the United States seizes them, their ship and cargo, with themselves, tramples on the territorial jurisdiction of the state of New York by seizing, disarming and sending on board their ship without warrant of arrest, several of them whom he found on shore, releases their captives, admits the claim of the two captives to the fifty masters as their slaves, and claims salvage for restoring them to servitude. They are then brought before a Court of the United States, at once upon the charge of piracy and murder, upon a claim to them as slaves and upon a claim against their pretended masters for salvage." He looked up from reading and grumbled loudly at the closing outhouse door. "You'd think if King Minos of Crete could have a flush toilet over 2,800 years ago, the Democrats, could get one in the nation's capital."

One cent was charged the curious at the jail show as admittance to see the Africans. Creating a line around the block and earning the jail three dollars and seventy-two cents the first day. Marshal Wilcox and his assistant Pendleton oversaw the Africans, in what they called, five apartments ... cells. Dr. Charles Hooker of New Haven attended them, six Mende were in a hospital apartment, four others were having trouble digesting the food they were not used to. The four children were in a room by themselves. Starting in the morning sight-seers passed through the jail and by the cells as a doctor and assistants made plaster casts of the Mende. In the background, an assistant and Dr. Fletcher took notes and measured the heads of several of the Blacks. Profiles were taken by a pentagraph from the casts. Dr. Moulthrop made a wax cast of one of the Africans. An assistant stirred more plaster. Louis Tappan watched the process, made some notes, opened the cell, and walked to the exit, pausing to hear some of the comments of the tourists.

"What kind o' heathen religion is they reverend?" a teenager asked the preacher helping Dr. Fletcher.

"They are giving themselves to God." He sighed.

A heavyset sailor puffing on a cigar leaned in close to the bars of the jail and elbowed the teenager, "Nah, before that they was cannibals."

"They were never cannibals," Tappan said too quickly.

"Ah, Ma, you said they's cannibals."

The mother looked flustered and quipped, "Well that's what the paper said. Pirates, killers, and cannibals."

The assistant measuring Pungwuni, turned, smirked, and answered, "Oh well, who among us has not sinned."

"The guard said they was Mo-ham-a-dans with fifty wives," said a young woman behind the sailor.

"I'm sure that is an exaggeration I would not know about. Two were formerly Muslims, but we are showing them the way to truth and life ever after. They have found God," the reverend smiled.

"That news about Mohammedans must have shocked the God-fearing abolitionists mightily."

"Tappan's a warden of his church."

"God help them," the second assistant laughed.

Tappan squeezed through the crowded doorway and walked outside. The line was long and was entertained by Ndamma playing a flute. Watching the others playing he held up a finger to tell Covey to wait a second. Ndamma finished his riff and started talking quickly, as much with his hands as words, bobbing his head to the group's beat while the line of tourists gossiped all sorts of odd and untrue facts about the Africans as if the Africans weren't there.

"We saw and conversed with the two Spanish gentlemen," one doctor said while waiting for a student to mix more plaster. "They were passengers on board the schooner, as well as owners of the Negroes and most of the cargo. One of them, Jose Ruiz, a very gentlemanly and intelligent young man, speaks English fluently."

"He's the owner of most of the slaves?"

"And the cargo. He was taking it to his estate in Cuba."

"He was taking them, not it." said the doctor.

"Right, anyhow, the other Spaniard, Pedro Montez, is old, what? about fifty and owned only three slaves."

"They'd of all sunk for sure if the *old guy* wasn't once a ship's master."

The doctor's assistant wrote notes as the doctor casually took measurements of Fuliwa and talked as if Fuliwa was just one of the plaster casts. His voice droned on as the jailer brought some steaming corn on the cob to the Africans. Because corn was new to them; the jailer took one of the hot ears, held it up gingerly, and chewed into it, showing them how to eat it. Waiting for the next tub of corn, six of the Africans set up a musical beat.

One of the Africans had cut a dozen three-inch-long tin strips of different width and stuck them into a foot long plank, making his version of a Kalimba then plucked a rhythm on it with his thumbs. Three others played elderberry flutes, another played a box with three strings stretched over it, another played a wood rasp, another played percussion on a tabletop. All this while the doctor studied a phrenology chart comparing the measurements he'd just taken while the band played.

Kwang ran his finger over the lines in the head on the chart and watched the doctor. Three assistants prepared more plaster as the doctor walked around Cinque, comparing his body with a printed chart, casually making notes out loud.

"Cinque's phrenological description is of a male about 26 years of age, of powerful frame, bilious and sanguine temperament, bilious predominating. His head by measurement is 22 3/8 inches in circumference, 15 inches from the root of the nose to the occipital protuberance over he top of the head, 15 inches from the Meatus Auditorious over the head, and 5 3/4 inches through the head at destructiveness. The development of the faculties is as follows: firmness; self-esteem; hope—very large. Benevolence; veneration; conscientiousness; approbativeness; wonder; concentrativeness; inhabitiveness; comparison; form—large. Amativeness; philoprogenitveness; adhesiveness; combativeness; destructiveness; secretiveness; constructiveness; caution; language; individuality; eventuality; causality; order—average. The head is well formed and such as a phrenologist admires. The coronal region being the largest, the frontal and occipital nearly balanced, and the basilar moderate. In fact, such an African head is seldom seen, and doubtless in other circumstances would have been an honor to his race. You can see by the interviews and statistics we have recorded here."

Curious, the Africans all handled and inspected the equipment as they were measured or plastered by the doctor and his assistants.

Having paid to see the captive Africans, tourists didn't seem to care who heard them say whatever came to mind, wondering out loud what the doctor was doing.

"Where they are from?"

"What do they eat?"

"Where do you exercise them?"

"How much they cost?"

"Are they for sale yet?"

"Were they neutered?"

"Do they sleep standing like horses?"

"That color come off?"

"There's no women. Don't they have women?"

"No wonder they went wild."

The outrageous questions are not meant to be hurtful, but would be if they were understood. The Africans were all together in the cell with the doctors. They talked and laughed about the shape, color, sound, and smell of the people looking at them.

The doctor and his team found Covey at the docks, an African who was taught by Jesuits. In the years before he joined the British navy, he translated for the Jesuit doctors and lawyers at the catholic compound. Covey, knew Portuguese, English, some Hebrew, two Latin prayers, and several Mende dialects. He translated for the Africans in jail awaiting trial. The doctor asked Cinque where he was from. Covey knew but asked the question exactly as the doctor asked.

"I was born in Mani in Dzhopoa, in Mende country. The distance from Mani to Lomboko is ten days. My mother is dead, I lived with my father."

Cinque explained how when he was walking along a path that he had taken hundreds of times with two of his children. They joked and listened to evening bird music, identifying each by their song. Then—as they came out of his field and started for home six men rushed out of the bush and jumped them. One of his children, who had stopped to watch a lizard, saw this and yelled a warning—too late. Two of the slavers ran after the children but the kids ran a serpentine path through the jungle and disappeared into the heavy foliage. Four slavers tied Cinque with a leather strip around his neck, with his arms pinned in back of him, Cinque was marched through his burning village.

"I have a wife and three children. I am a planter of rice. I was seized by six men, when returning home, and my hands tied. They burned my village and took many from there. Maya Gilalo sold me to Bamadzha, son of Shaka, King of Genduma in Vai country. I and many from different villages were sold at Lomboko to a Spaniard."

Lomboko. Bloody chains, sweaty hot sun, hard shadows. A dozen trails lead to the fort. Lomboko was a fortified slave store in Sierra Leone. It was responsible for hundreds of thousands of slaves shipped to the Americas. It was rife with chikungunya, dengue fever, hepatitis, malaria, measles, polio, rabies, tetanus, tuberculosis, typhoid, and yellow fever. It was ruled by a Spanish slaver, ironically named Pedro Blanco. The fort was surrounded by guards patrolling a high stone wall. Several large holding depots, called barracoons were full of slaves arriving daily from the interior. There were four palatial buildings where Blanco kept his favorite concubines and workers. The trails leading to the fort and the river were constantly filled with chained slaves being led in long lines down to a pier where several ships under different flags waited for oncoming slaves. The Amistad survivors were linked together harsh and fast.

Covey started his questions with Cinque while Grabeau hung on every word. "Grabeau, was born at Fulu, in Mende country. He seemed to be the next, after Cinque, in command of the Amistad. His parents were dead, one brother and one sister were living, he thinks. He is married, but no children; he was a planter of rice. His king Baw-baw, lived at Fulu. He was caught on the road going to buy clothes in Taurang, in the Bandi country, His uncle had bought two slaves in Bandi, and gave them in payment for a debt; one of them ran away, so Grabeau was taken as a replacement for him. He was sold to a Vai-man who sold him to a Portuguese, who sold him to Laigo, a Spaniard at Lomboko. Grabeau is four feet eleven inches in height; very active. Besides Mende, he speaks Vai, Konno, and Gissi. He aided John Ferry by his knowledge of Gissi, in his examination at Hartford."

"Kimbo 5'6" in height, with full Mustaches, and beard; in middle life, and intelligent. He was born at Mawkoba, a town in the Mende country. His father was a gentleman, and after his death, his king took him for his slave, and gave him to his son Banga, residing in the Bullom country. He was sold to a Bullom man, who sold him to a Spaniard at Lomboko."

"Konnoma 5'4" in height, proud of his large lips and projecting mouth, his incisor teeth press outward and are filed because he says—women like this. He is tattooed in the forehead with a diamond shape. He was born in the Konno country." His dialect was not readily under-stood by Covey. He knew some Mandingo vocabulary.

"Burna 5'2". He was a blacksmith in Mende. He was sold for a crime. He does not want to talk about it," Covey added, "Not surprising he does not want to speak of it, because blacksmiths are not supposed to be taken in war, or as slaves. It is surprising, I thought it was law.

"Bartu 5'6" with a tattooed breast, born in Tuma by Mawua lake. His father is a gentleman and does not work. His king, Dabe, resided in Tuma. He was sent to the village by his father and was seized by six men. He was ten days travel to Lomboko. He says there are high mountains in his country, near Sierra Leone.

"Gnakwoi. Born in Konggolahung in Balu country by the Zaliba river. He was on a trip to the gold country and was taken by a gang of Balu men.

"Kwong. Born in Mambui in Mende country. He and his wife were sold for a debt by his landowner to a Spaniard at Lomboko.

"Fuliwa. Born in Mano, he lived with his parents and five brothers. His town was surrounded and attacked by soldiers; some soldiers were killed. He, with his brothers and two sisters in-law in the village were taken prisoner.

"Pie A Timmani. A hunter. He and his son were captured on the road by Vai men. That's all he will say.

"Pungwuni 5'1". Body tattooed, teeth filed, was born in Febaw in Sando. His uncle sold him for a coat. He was sold to Garloba he stayed there for two years, then was sold to Spaniards."

Moru noded at Sessi and started to tell his story. They all stood by the ruler that the doctor put on the wall, then circled around Covey, listening to the stories of before the Amistad.

"Sessi 5'7". Born in Massakum, in Bandi country. He is a blacksmith. He was taken captive by soldiers and wounded in the leg. His village was burned. He saw his wife and baby die there in his house. He says his mother was laying on the floor, her white hair was red. Her eyes open, she saw everything no more. He was sold twice before he was taken to Lomboko.

"Moru 5'8". Born at Sanka, in Bandi country. His parents died when he was a child. His master, Margona sold him to buy his tenth wife.

"Ndamma 5'3" Born in Mende on the river Male. He was taken on the road by—he proudly pounds his chest—it took 20 men.

"Fuliwulu Born in Timmani near Mende country he is the son of Pie.

"Bau 5'5". He was caught coming home by 8 men as he was coming from planting rice; His grandfather and mother were killed. He saw their legs sticking out of his doorway. His wife and child were beaten and tied. They were all taken to Lomboko. He saw them sold.

"Ba 5'4". He was captured on the way to gather cattle by two men and sold to a Via man who sold him to Spaniards.

"Shule 5'4". The oldest of the Amistad captives, born at Konabu, in Mende. Momawru caught both him and his master Maya, and made them slaves.

"Berri 5'3". Was born in Fangte in Gula, a large, fenced town, where his king, Gelewa resided. He was sold to Shaka, king of Genduma, in the Vai or Gallina country, who sold him to a Spaniard. Genduma, nine miles from the sea, is on a river called Boba.

"Kali, Tcmc, Kagne, and Margru are children. All were sold to pay off debts of their families."

The doctor finished writing and looked up at Covey. "Just for the record we should have you on record too."

Covey laughed out loud, "Me? Ha-ha-ha. I am James Covey, the interpreter for the Africans—Ahhh, all right, I am 20 years old. I was born at Benderi, in the Mende country. My father was of Konno descent, my mother Gissi. As a child I was taken by three men. Before my purification, called biriye, before my ritual was held. Before the cleansing ushers a child into adulthood. Then, as a man, one is expected to take on a man's responsibilities. I did not know what tribe my abductors were. It was night, at Golahung. I was sold to the king of the Bulloms in Mani.

I was kept there for three years and sold to a Portuguese living near Mani who carried me with 300 others to Lomboko. We were put on a Portuguese slave ship and four days out of Lomboko, boarded by a British armed vessel before the Portuguese could hook our chain to an anchor and push us all overboard. We were taken to Sierra Leone. I was given my freedom, and remained there for five years and was taught to read and write English and Latin in the church mission. I enlisted as a sailor on board the British brig of war—Buzzard. It was on board this vessel, when at New York, in Oct. 1839 that I was found and, by the kindness of Captain Fitzgerald, allowed to offer my services as an interpreter."

CHAPTER TEN

New York City

Returning from a fund raiser in Boston with Simeon Joceyln, and Joshua Leavitt, Tappan dodged across a bustling New York City street, avoiding a rotting horse carcass at the curb. The city was crowded with coaches and trade wagons; the traffic jam was a mess. Carefully maneuvering around a hundred thousand horses, manure, urine, and someone's chamber pot leavings, he was on his way to his office. He stopped to buy an apple. Across the street several men who had been waiting for him shouted to four other men who charged cross the street and started yelling over the street noise.

"There's Tappan! Get him. Get the nigger lover."

One man knocked Tappan's apple out of his hand as he tried to wrestle him to the street. Tappan managed to shove the first man into a water trough and ran zigzagging through horses, coaches, and traffic. More anti-abolitionists joined the mob and chased Tappan three blocks to his warehouse. Slam! He jumped inside and bolted the new iron door. Crash! A stone shattered the glass in the front, now bared, window. The side door was battered with an old iron conestoga wagon jack until it finally splintered and crashed in. Tappan grabbed the printer's devil and shoved him out the back door. They ran through the alley as the furious mob of thirty surged into his office and scattered, ripped, and burnt everything in sight.

The Grampus was anchored in New York harbor, detached from the African Squadron, her next assignment would be the protection of shipping in the Caribbean. Lieutenant Pain leaned against a swivel cannon on the Grampus, watching two junior officers walk from dock to deck with a senior officer who had just hand-delivered a message. They looked curiously at the Lieutenant and started asking questions before he had fully scanned the document.

"A warrant of the President of the United States?!"

"It's for you, it says—'Attention to Lieutenant Pain, commander of the Grampus. Hereby to receive and convey the Negroes of the Amistad, to Cuba, 7, January 1840, in the custody of the Marshall, under process pending before the Circuit court."

"The secretary of state told the District Attorney: that if the decision of the court isn't what they anticipate, then he has to carry out that order of the President."

"What about the court?"

"Well damnation, he is the president," a junior officer laughed.

"Can't the president do what he wants?"

"Well. You can't not do what the judge tells you," the deck officer added.

"Well Jesus! Sir... Who's in charge?" The confused junior officer looked back and forth between his two superior officers.

"The Secretary of State has to do what the judge says," Pain shook his head and handed the parchment to the junior officer.

The second junior officer tried not to laugh. "Even Van Buren can't tell the judge to do something illegal."

Pain sighed, "Yes. But Van Buren can tell the Navy."

"No, he can't tell us to do something illegal," the senior officer said.

"The President knows Hollabird ordered the marshal to deliver them to the control of the Navy." The officer cleared his throat trying to not laugh at the younger officer's expression.

"Van Buren instructed Hollabird not to place the vessel's cargo or the slaves outside the jurisdiction of the Federal Executive. No legal argument would prevail IF Judge Judson accepted the President's orders. You can bet that infuriated Adams and the Constitutionalists."

"Well, they're not American are they."

"Well, they do have that against them."

"Ha, the Spanish Ambassador can't understand how the president of the United States can be told what to do by a mere judge," Pain laughed.

The junior officer shuffled through 4 pages and looked up, "So if the court does order the slaves back to Cuba, the President's not going to allow time for an appeal."

"Grab them and run." The deck officer pointed at the parchment writ. "So! Here is an order from the President—to the marshal of the district, directing him to place the Negroes at your disposition. Another for the district attorney for the United States, W.S. Hollabird. And finally, a letter to the Council de Havana stating you will assist the 'Spanish minister as efficiently and speedily as possible' from Secretary of State J. Forsyth."

"And we follow orders."

"Wait a minute sir. This ship isn't big enough for forty passengers and their guards."

"Well, it's bigger than the one they came on."

Pain was not happy. "In January? On deck? Storms would be disastrous."

"Well lieutenant, treat them with all possible tenderness and attention."

"Sir, I don't—the Navy doesn't run slave ships," Pain snapped.

"Try telling that to Van Buren, sir," the young ensign repined.

"Or the court." Pain folded the parchment and shoved it in his coat pocket.

The deck officer looked out to the bay at the mass of incoming and outgoing ships' sails billowing in the wind.

"Be careful lieutenant. We're sailing in very dangerous waters there."

"Isn't that what you said just before we survived the Drake Passage sir."

"Ha those were only forty-foot waves."

February 24th, 1841

The eagle on the wall was mostly in shadow now—daylight just touching it. A band played outside, accompanied by the sounds of street traffic and food vendors. People stepped aside for Clay, whose deep Virginian accent and direct way of speaking, honed in law school, cleared his path.

Always a gentleman in mixed company, he easily could sling mud with the worst. And all here knew he survived his latest duel with senator Randolph, who at a party called Clay a diseased bull. The tradition of the day dictated that Randolph's utterances on the floor could not be used to demand a duel. Senators were allowed then to say whatever they wanted about political rivals on the Senate floor and not face gunfire. A good policy, because we'd have never-ending elections, and slander is better than revolvers, Bowie knives, and street assassinations with the lie of self-defense.

But today Clay is escorting his wife, Lucretia Hart Clay into the Court, explaining the first act of the grand play now unfolding in the courtroom. "Ahh, the room is crowded with genteel women, finely dressed, and there's the gentlemen of Washington, and Boston, and another New Yorker and four from New Orleans and Atlanta. Where else could they hear language or see drama like this. Even the melodrama of theater lacks the power of the true emotions vented here. There are few writers in the world who can put words into the mouths of this caliber of action."

The crowd pushed in and settled down. The act started. A newspaperman wrote quickly, stopped, looked up and leaned over to his companion newsman and murmured, "This is really a clear challenge to Judge Judson."

His companion noisily flipped a page in his pad and wrote faster, "Will he take the challenge or submit to the President?"

Atkin, the artist sitting with them, looked back and forth from his charcoal pad to the animated subjects in the courtroom arguing, cajoling, and threatening each other right in front of him. He smirked "Or will Jenson hold the Constitution against the blatant interference from Van Buren?"

"Hollabird won't stop at this challenge." The newspapermen looked over at the drawing and then up at the judge, "His nose is too big."

"The nose is right, his head is too small."

"You just try and spell your little quotes right, I'll do the pictures," the artist growled. All three must interrupt their work, gather up their papers, and stand to let two men and a woman pass by them to get to the last three empty chairs. Holding their work to their chests they watched two more go past them and then past the three who just entered and there was no empty chair, so they had to edge their way back, with everyone standing as the two went by saying, sorry, sorry, sorry. The room fast became full to standing room only.

"Obviously slave owners in the South are up in arms about this case," the first newsman whispers, trying to hear what the bailiff and marshal are saying.

"They say it could kill the future of slavery where it had been legal for years. Some even conjure visions of armed slaves runnin' North to freedom in droves."

The woman who just walked by them turns, smiles primly, and says, "Those ol' Yankee abolitionists say the Africans gotta be freed, and the US must not interfere on behalf of the slave holders. Isn't that just so mean?"

February 26th, 1841

A smiling Adams attended the funeral of Judge Barbour at Washington's Eastern Branch Cemetery, with a bruised and bandaged James who eased out of the coach and followed slowly. Watching them was an accumulation from all faiths; Southern, Yankee, Republican, Jeffersonians, Democrat, old

Whigs, Tired Tories, anti-abolitionists, abolitionists, and an assortment of people cursing him because they just didn't like the damned old man. Adams waved a rather wilted arrangement of flowers at them all in the cold afternoon sun.

Although he was a Jackson man, the deceased judge Barbour had decided that people could not be considered commerce. Nationalists had feared Jackson's appointment of Barbour because Barbour's anti-administration Democratic attitude would undermine the federal supremacy achieved during Marshall's leadership. On March 15th, 1836, the Senate approved the appointment of Barbour by a vote of 30-11. During his brief term on court, Barbour heard 155 cases, for which he authored one major opinion and two dissents. Although Justice Barbour only served on the Supreme Court for five years, he became an active agent in shaping states' rights and strict reading of the Constitution to place limits on federal power.

As JQ Adams approached the assembled they all turned their backs on him. Adams poked James in the ribs and chuckled, "Ah, look at them James. If General Washington wouldn't appoint a friend because he was a friend, or remove an enemy, Jackson changed all that by removing anyone with an idea, and replacing him with a dollar. Spoils, young James; to the victor belongs the spoils."

"And they are all spoiled," James grumbled.

"What the president has done threatens to destroy our system of law." "An act of desperation, sir."

"He's afraid of the Supreme Court."

"He's got no respect for law."

Adams turned and walked to his coach. "Hmph. This is a government of laws James, not men. Though some are too quick to forget."

The priest stepped to the grave, waved his hand over the descending casket and mumbled words that were too cold to reach past the clouds of his breath. All assembled have their heads down wondering what the hell they can do to overcome those opposing powers of the assembled around them—except representative Henry Wise, pro-union, pro slavery, pro national bank, and a duel survivor—he called Adams "The acutest, the astutest, archest enemy of southern slavery that ever existed."

A group of Yale students and James Covey sat in a circle at the jailhouse teaching the Africans to read English. They were all assembled in one of the jail cells, pointing at lithographs and woodcuts of American towns, landscapes and still-life pictures of African villages from Lander's Travels. The Africans were quick to try their English.

"In Mende country no white man," Kimbo said, and pointed at an etching.

"So, Winterbottom's excursion never got to the interior then?" a student wondered. "What about your village?"

"Snow?" another student asked.

Bartu smiled and nodded, "Little, little. Not so much as here."

"Were you a chief?"

Bartu laughed, "Me? Ha-ha, no, no, no."

Nghoni pointed at the chief's carved chair in a picture. "Chief father, chief son, and sons, be son chief."

"Who is over chief?"

"Shaka king. All people give to king. Every new moon all bring—rich and poor bring to Shaka king," Barri said proudly.

Cinque asked, "Here the same?"

"Our great man is elected." The doctor pointed at the flag.

"Every one gets together and chooses," one of the students added .

"Oh?" A curious question flickered across Cinque's face, thinking that was a lot to ponder.

The jailer, who leaned against the cell door added, "In a democracy everyone chooses chief."

Berri mumbled, "This word—De-mo-cracy?"

One of the students nodded, "Every four years we choose Great Man." "Four years?" Burner pronounces the words carefully.

Cinque laughed—then they all laughed.

"King is for life, own everything. Baby, woman, man, everybody. No one tell king what to do. Very strange is democracy."

Berri shook his head. "This thing can not work."

The doctor added. "We had that problem once. We kicked the king out. Big fight. But Democracy won. No king here."

All the Africans looked at one another wide eyed—not believing.

A dozen sailboats were just visible in the early morning Potomac river mist, anchored close into the river's shore. Their rigging knocked quietly as they rocked with the flow of the river. Adams started his swim against the current so the return would be easier. In the distance Jeremy sat smoking his pipe in the coach while Antoine waited on the shore with Adams's greatcoat and clothes.

"Adams turned, changed to a floating slow backstroke, and rehearsed the facts in his court room voice, "Spanish minister, I have admitted that the principles which maybe are supposed to govern him might go far to justify the sympathy he has shown for one party exclusively. But I cannot give the same credit for the sympathy shown by our own government. In this letter we meet, for the first time, something that might appear like sympathy for the poor wretches whose liberties and lives were in peril.

"Here is a desire intimated that they might go to Cuba, for the purpose of having an opportunity to prove in the courts of Spain their right to be free by the laws of Spain.

And the President, in the abundance of his kindness, orders Lieutenants Gedney and Meade to be sent along with them, as witnesses in the case, 'particularly,' the Secretary said, 'with regard to the real condition of the negroes,' that is, whether they were free or slaves. But what did Lieutenants Gedney and Meade know about that? They could testify to nothing but the circumstances of the capture.

"And as to the other idea, that these people should have an opportunity to prove their freedom in Cuba, how could that be credited as a motive, when it is apparent that, by sending them back in the capacity of slaves, they would be deprived of all power to give evidence at all in regard to their freedom! I cannot, therefore, give the Executive credit for this sympathy towards the Africans. It was a mere pretense, to blind the public mind with the idea that the Africans were merely sent to Cuba to prove they were not slaves. So far from giving any credit for this sympathy, the letter itself furnishes incontestable evidence of a very different disposition, which I will not qualify in words.

"Pursuing the case chronologically, according to the course of the proceedings, I now call the attention of the Court to the opinion of the late Attorney General of the United States, which the Secretary of the State told Mr. Argaiz had been adopted by the Cabinet, and which has been the foundation, to this day, of all the proceedings of the Executive in the case. Before considering this, however,

I will advert to the letter of Messrs. Staples and Sedgwick to the President. These gentlemen were counsel for those unfortunate men. There had been reports in circulation, which is by no means surprising, considering the course of the public sympathy, that the President intended to remove these people to Cuba, by force, *gubernativamente*, by virtue of his Executive authority—that inherent power which I suppose has been discovered, by which the President, at his discretion, can seize men, and imprison them, and send them beyond seas for trial or punishment by a foreign power."

Adams gasped out loud, "Lord it is cold., as he bargained with God. "This is your servant from Quincy Lord—*gasp*—Just—give me the strength—to make it to that warm far shore. We have traveled a long and flinty road together Lord—We have seen this country given over to every force of greed and hate and ignorance. Your servant Lord. Your enemies are my own—*gasp*.

"You gave us the freedom to think.It's a fight for freedom. Freedom from the shackles in the South. Freedom to petition in Congress. Freedom for the human mind in knowledge and science. There is no compromise Lord; sink or swim. I shall fight Your enemies Lord—*gasp*—with my back to the wall. Fight for freedom, and compassion arghh! Though you might consider a little warm comfort to fortify your helpmates. Gasp! The forcible arrest of these men, or a part of them, on the soil of New York, was wrong. After the vessel was brought into the jurisdiction of the District Court of Connecticut, the men were first scized—*gasp*—and imprisoned under a criminal process for murder and piracy on the high seas. Then they were libeled by Lt. Gedney, as property, and he claimed them as salvage– ahh, praise be, the shore arrives."

CHAPTER ELEVEN

The house floor is always full of dealmakers making deals. Senator Walker was waiting angrily for one. He spit, missed the spittoon: a bad omen. So he cursed two aides, and five House members, in the group around him. They all turned to glare at Adams.

The oldest aide, sixteen, leaned to the younger, fourteen, and wondered, "So, John Quincy Adams, it's said, belonged to neither of the prominent political parties, fights no partisan battles, and cannot be prevailed upon to sacrifice truth and principle upon the altar of party expediency and interest. Hence, neither party is interested in defending his course, or in giving him an opportunity to defend himself. Why?"

The younger lad shrugged.

Still, John Quincy Adams pressed on. In time he received from some of his colleagues the nickname "Old Man Eloquent", Others, less charitable, called him "That God damned Adams." He had been presenting anti-slavery petitions in the House for almost four years. In early 1836, these petitions became ever more numerous, reaching the tens of thousands. Abolitionists capitalized on the right to petition as a vital method of protest against southern state governments and the Jackson administration, both of which endorsed and even assisted in stifling the spread of abolitionist literature.

Fuming at the deluge of petitions, South Carolina's John Henry Hammond moved that any petition with a slavery topic be discarded "peremptorily," and not noted. A very animated debate erupted in the House over the constitutional right to petition. After a week of heated discussion and flying accusations, a compromise committee was formed. After almost four months the 'compromise committee' presented these three resolutions: 1. That Congress was not constitutionally authorized to legislate against slavery in southern states. 2. That Congress "ought not" legislate against slavery in the District of Columbia. And 3. That any petition even remotely related to the topic of slavery be automatically banned from mention or discussion in the House.

The resolutions were passed in a gesture of "compromise" and pacification to calm southern tension about abolishing slavery. But true to form, John Quincy Adams saw no compromise. He viewed the first two resolutions as misguided and flawed deductions of constitutional law; the third, which became known as the "gag rule" was a blatant contravention of the Bill of Right's guarantee of the right to petition. As if called to battle Adams began a campaign against the resolutions, attacking them at every opportunity and challenging their legality.

Old man eloquent had spent years in the trenches learning the machinery of government and masterfully manipulated the House at every opportunity to attack the gag rule. Essentially alone, and despite his fearless attacks, his opponents were able to pass a standing gag rule in 1840. Despite this he constantly suckered southern

Congressmen into debates on slavery sometimes lasting for days.

In all House proceedings, Adams was joyfully condescending, controversial, and cutting, using every arcane, esoteric rule at his disposal to achieve his objective to generate debates on slavery. He intentionally baited irate House members to censure him for his conduct. When they did, he employed the time granted him for defense to expound his views on slavery-related issues. On one such occasion, Adams spoke for two weeks on his defense and threatened to go on for another two weeks unless the House tabled the censure resolution against him. The resolution was tabled, and Adams emerged doubly successful, for he had used those two weeks to denounce slaveholders for abusing slaves as well as free abolitionists, whose constitutional rights of petition, speech, and the press had been circumscribed.

Gray day, gray drizzle, gray street. Adams hurried to the coach in the downpour as James splashed along beside him. Adams pontificated about the southern bloc. "Patton's one of the ablest, most independent, and most rational of the slaveholding members,"

"And that's not sayin' a lot."

"Now James."

"Nevertheless, was it not Patton who stated that any member who presented a petition from slaves ought to be considered an enemy of the Union. A traitor!"

"Patton's resolution conflicts with the Constitution, because the Constitution affirms that treason against the United States shall consist *only* in levying war against us, or adhering to our *enemies*, giving them aid and comfort."

"But Patton demanded any member ought to be considered an enemy for presenting such a petition."

"That, James, is violation of freedom of speech."

With a rhetorical flourish, Adams later wrote to his constituents: "If such a question as I asked of the Speaker is a direct invitation of the slaves to insurrection, forfeiting all my rights as a representative of the people, subjecting me to indictment by a grand jury, to conviction by a petit jury, and to an infamous penitentiary cell—I ask you not what freedom of speech is left to your representative in Congress, but what freedom of speech, of the press, and of thought, is left to you?"

The resolution called for "all petitions, memorials, resolutions, propositions, or papers, relating in any way, or to any extent whatever, to the subject of slavery, or the abolition of slavery, shall, without being either printed or referred, be laid upon the table, and that no action whatever shall be had thereon."

It was a continuing frustration to Adams that at every turn there was bickering and opposition to him. But all in attendance were sure the old man enjoyed his aggravation of the government, so he continued objection of his tabling, and their thwarting of his petitions. When Adams began to read a petition calling for abolition of slavery in the District of Columbia a storm of protests erupted from the chambers: "Order, Order."

A query from Patton, on whether the rules permitted members to read petitions, was firmly put forward by Polk. "It is not in order for a member to read a petition, whether it was long or short, one can only make a brief statement of the contents."

Adams smirked that that was outrageous, "Who ever heard of such a rule—that a member of the House should not have the power to read what he chose. It's an absurdity, because my brief statement of the contents is so short, that to read the petition in its own language was the briefest statement that could be made."

Polk didn't like it at all, because of the opposition of the southern states. They thought the right to petition helped focus the public on slavery.

"Judas priest, it's an unending river of petitions," Glasscock spit out his words like a vile taste. "No, Goddamn it, it's a deluge! Adams's flooding the floor with petitions!" He turned to glare at Old Man Eloquent who was rising to speak.

Adams cleared his throat, "Mr. Speaker. It was my intention to move to lay the petition on the table. Has it been received?"

"It has not."

Glasscock blurted out angrily, "Nay! Mr. Speaker, I say it should not."

Adams retorted with a wave of the hand, "I know of no law, except the Declaration of Independence... that reaches the case of my clients but the Law of Nature and of Nature's God on which our fathers placed our own national existence."

90 members shouted, "Yes!" They grouped together; some pointed at Adams, some shook their fists. All argued in a babble of shouts and banged their fists or anything else that was handy on their desks as the Speaker pounded his gavel. Nine pushed against each other to fit in the aisle as they charged down the aisle to be blocked by John Quincy Adams's aides. Sixty members yelled. The speaker tried again, "Point of order. Point of order, Point of order!"

Some threw up their hands in exasperation. Others walked out. Several sat and poured stiff shots from their flasks and their flask canes and shook their heads in bewilderment. The entire House seemed to be against Adams.

Every day Adams swam against the early morning current with an effort. The water's strength caused wakes around boats pulling at their anchor lines. The only thing heard above the rattling of the boat's masts was the voice of John Adams arguing with God about the world He's leaving behind for Adams to agitate.

The mist cleared and birds were just starting to be seen and heard.

"Stay with me Lord.—*gasp*—We can do it. A little strength against the tide Lord. It's your fault you know! It's your doing. You're the one who gave us thought. Freedom of the mind—in knowledge and science. Freedom of ideas. Ha! Yes! Who was the Spanish owner here with his ship?!?

"There was none!" he sputtered. "The Africans were here with their ship. You say the original owner was Spanish? He's dead, and cannot claim benefit of all this—but the Africans can claim salvage. So, ha-ha-ha, It's now an African vessel. Gasp! And yet, you say, they did not bring the vessel into our waters. Truth is they were deceived, against their will, by the two Spaniards. Lord! but it's cold here in the heat of battle." The coach can just be seen as Adams propels his way to shore. James and Antoine stood waiting patiently with John Adams's long coat and towel.

Bright and early that day Adams stood to speak, smiled, and then calmly, without notes—in about thirty seconds caused pandemonium to break out. A new record for him. "A petition of the citizens of Dedham in the state of Massachusetts praying Congress immediately adopt measures, peaceably, to dissolve the Union of these States, for three reasons which I set forth in this petition."

Then the uproar. Chapman shouted to adjourn, Houston also; they were refused. Turney tried to make a motion, Halbersham also was refused after he managed to be heard, then everyone, not just the slavocracy started shouting.

James rushed through the corridor leaving two other aides to protect Adams. Aiming for the doors at the end of the hall where several news men were congregated, he grabbed John Greenleaf Whittier. Speaking rapidly he blurted out, "A petition calling for the dissolution of the Union was put forward by Mister Adams." That outrage worked. The roar filling the hall was accompanied by a near riot in the House, causing nearly two weeks of very loud debate. The press on all sides joined in the outrage. However Congress did not execute its motion to censure.

Then a week later: "Mr. Speaker I have several petitions."

Almost before Adams opened his mouth the slaveocracy started its brouhaha.

Knowing what was coming, the Speaker interrupted Adams.

"Mr. Adams, the special committee, of which Mr. H. L. Pinckney is chairman for three months, declared that Congress has no power to interfere with slavery in any state; that it ought not to interfere with it in the District of Columbia; and, since discussion of the topic is so disquieting, all petitions regarding it should in the future be laid on the table without being printed or referred and without any further action being taken on them. The vote was 182 to 9."

Adams shouts over the din. "That, mister Speaker is a false document and against all meanings of democracy and freedom of speech. A direct violation of the Constitution of the United States, the rules of this house and the rights of my constituents!"

"Order! Order! Order"

"I shall continue to petition the House. I have here 22 persons who stated that they were slaves."

The floor erupts. Adams stops, looks around, sees Benton and smiles. He sits, waits, listening to the familiar shouts.

"Point of order!"

"Treason!"

"Censure."

"Expel Adams."

Adams rose slowly; smiling, like an actor listening to shouts of encore.

But Benton stood quickly and pounded on his desk, shouting, "It is well known, abolitionist Adams has introduced petitions ad nauseam for the abolition of slavery."

Congress was up again and shouting, banging mugs on desks, and stomping.

Adams's aides braced themselves.

Thompson started up again. "Treason! Treason, treason, treason!"

Walker, red faced, veins popping, shouted, "Adams oughta be hauled before the Grand Jury in tar and feathers!"

Thompson laughed, "He would be if he were in South Carolina!"

"Thank God I am not a citizen in South Carolina. Are we from the Northern States to be indicted as felons and incendiaries, for presenting petitions not agreeable to some members from the South? You have mistaken me sir, I am not to be intimidated by you or all the Grand Juries of the universe. Mister speaker—I here present three hundred and fifty petitions, praying that Congress will take measures to protect citizens of the North going to the South from danger to their lives."

As the yelling got louder, Adams waited. Clay watched, worried. Henry Clay served as secretary of state under President John Quincy Adams and knew how easily Adams could rouse the less than righteous to battle.

Adams shook his head. "In another part of the Capitol it has been threatened that if a Northern abolitionist should go to North Carolina and utter any principle of the Declaration of Independence..."

Again, shouts. More banging for of order, order. The Speaker banged his gavel.

The floor bustled with people arguing.

Adams, the lightning rod, continued "...that if they could catch him they would hang him."

A chant starts up, "Order! Order!"

The Speaker continued to bang his gavel, "Will the Goddamned gentleman from Massachusetts take his seat."

Adams sat, rose again, and slowly looked around the hall. "I have here mister Speaker another petition."

"Order, order," started up again.

"Mister Adams there was a vote before the house. You will answer merely Aye, or No when asked for a vote in connection to this vote."

Adams sighed, "I refuse to answer so, because I consider all the current proceedings of the House as unconstitutional."

"Order, order."

"Treason!"

"This is all a direct violation of the Constitution of the United States," Adams said as loudly and as nonchalantly as he could. A fight broke out on the back benches as both sides yelled. The speaker franticly scanned the room for the House Marshal and yelled over the chaos, banging his gavel with passion. Clay, a big man, waded through the morass to John Quincy's desk.

Clay was a War Hawk, aggressive, full of words and none of them too subtle. He actively harassed the president and congress to intervene in the illegal taking of American seamen who were being pressed into the British navy. Clay played no little part in America going to war in 1812. Strangely he was also one of the delegates to forge a peace treaty. When the battles ceased, President James Madison had appointed Clay as one of five delegates to negotiate a peace treaty with Britain in Ghent, Belgium.

Clay pushed for a national bank and argued to negotiate the Missouri Compromise in 1820 between slave states and the rest of the country setting western policy, which allowed for America to expand westward—without the volatile topic of slavery.

As a private citizen, Clay was a very successful attorney. One of his many clients was Aaron Burr. Clay represented Burr in 1806 in a stranger than fiction case that claimed Burr was planning an expedition into Spanish Territory to create a new empire. The alleged cabal of over forty thousand was to be led by Aaron Burr, former Vice President of the United States. He was accused of planning to create an independent country in the middle of what was to become the United States. General James Wilkinson was one of Burr's key partners, who was the commanding general of the United States army, known for his attempt to separate Kentucky and Tennessee from the union. Burr persuaded President Thomas Jefferson to appoint Wilkinson to the position of Governor of the Louisiana Territory. Wilkinson would later send a letter to Jefferson that Wilkinson claimed was evidence of Burr's treason.

While Burr was still Vice President, he met with Anthony Merry, the British Minister to the United States. Burr told Merry that the British might regain power in the Americas because the Southwest was open for the taking—if they contributed guns and money for his plan of detaching Louisiana from the Union. The price for the exchange was half a million dollars and the protection of the British fleet.

In his communication to Great Brittan Merry wrote, "It is clear Mr. Burr means to endeavor to be the instrument for effecting such a connection. He has told me that the inhabitants of Louisiana prefer having the protection and assistance of Great Britain."

Even after all this, Burr was not found guilty of treason, he was never convicted, there was no hard evidence, no conclusive testimony. The star witness admitted he had doctored the letter incriminating Burr. It seems the invasion of Spanish lands or secession of American territory was not considered treasonous in view of the unsecured and unsettled southwestern borders at the time. That and the belief of President Jefferson and others was that the United States seemed destined to divide into at least two nations. Acquitted of treason the trial however destroyed Burr's political career, Clay refused to speak to Burr after the trial. Clay was again battling on the floor of Congress; that was America to him.

The Room was in an uproar. The speaker threw down his gavel and shouted. "Goddammit, I call upon the House to support me in the execution of my duty!"

In what became a nearly daily routine, Clay, ironically called "the great Pacifier," helped three battered aides hold back ten congressmen from attacking Adams. Trying to avoid the six-foot four Clay, the group of men pushed and shoved in the aisles around Adams, who continued undeterred. "Not true. I am not an abolitionist. I hold no abolitionist office. You say that the Negroes named in my petitions are of a low sort. I adhere to the right of petition. Petition is prayer! And where is the decree which shall deprive any citizen the right to pray for mercy? Where is such a law to be found? The sultan of Constantinople cannot walk the streets and refuse to receive petitions from the meanest and vilest in the land. The right belongs to all."

Back in the Potomac again, the river, like the Southern block, pushed against Adams every day, a lone, small figure, fighting the opposing forces. "You gave us a curious mind God; you let us think—*gasp*—Well, most of us. Search for the light, do not hide behind the veil of darkness—*gasp*—Take me over the river Lord. Give me the strength to finish the battle—*gasp*—My own district and state is convulsed between slavery and abolition, and yeah, I walk on the edge of a precipice every step I take."

Naked in the steaming cold river, Adams dragged himself out of the water.

Antoine threw a heavy coat around him and they hurried to the coach.

Later that morning the sun cast long shadows along the street as Jeremy let Adams out of the carriage at the steps of the Capital building and continued on. Four Native Americans, one older and wearing beads, the others younger and dressed as any of the men about them, stepped forward. Luther Peck shook John's hand.

"Mornin' Mr. Adams."

"Ah, good morning, Mr. Peck. Your friends?"

"Yes, we thought it safer if we catch you out here, before you got caught up in the pyrotechnics."

"Hm, pyrotechnics? Just another day of democracy in action."

As they walked up the marble stairs Peck introduced the Native Americans. Two men argued, shouting at each other face to face at the entrance of the House.

"That's Garret Davis of Kentucky's replying to Johnson. He's beyond calling him a liar, a fraud, and coward. That's a hazard of the profession."

"Unbelievable. Uncivilized," Peck stared at Adams in disbelief.

"Well, this is Mr. Pierce who is going to Dartmouth college, and Mr. Two Guns. We want to talk to you about presenting their petition, on the fraudulent treaty to herd the Seneca from their homes like swine."

Passers-by glared at them as they walked up the marble stairs, entered the heavy doors, and passed into the outer chambers crowded with angry gossiping citizens and members of the House arriving and departing and asserting their way through the crowd.

The doors crashed open and a loud gang of congressmen shoved their way into the incoming crowd. One white-haired congressman was bludgeoning a much younger man with his cane. Several rolled on the floor while a dozen others swung wildly. A spittoon flew through the door, banged against a marble statue of Eirene, a young lady carrying a cornucopia, a torch and a scepter—the goddess of peace. Shouts of nigger lover, abolitionist, damn Yankee, white trash, redneck, hillbilly, son of a bitch, whoremonger, merge with a hundred other worse curses. Dozens of men ran to join sides. The three native Americans looked on stoically. Two Gun stepped gingerly back from the struggling mob, "This is the White man's law?"

"This is worse than, Arapaho, Pawnee wars," Peck pointed at the altercation and exclaimed in disbelief.

CHAPTER TWELVE

Adams strode through the halls while shuffling sheaves of papers in some kind of order. He glanced at his two aides, stopped, turned to them and in his annoyingly calm sarcastic-sounding voice tested his theme on them.

"The whole of my argument to show that the appeal should be dismissed, is founded on an averment that the proceedings on the part of the United States are all wrongful—from the beginning. The first act of seizing the vessel, and these men, by an office of the Navy, was wrong." Adams smiled a crooked little smile. "The forcible arrest of these men, or a part of them, on the soil of New York, was wrong. After—the vessel was brought into the jurisdiction of the District Court of Connecticut, the men were seized and then imprisoned under a criminal process for murder and piracy on the high seas."

Adams handed a fist-full of pages to James as he plowed into the crowded hall. His aides scurried to keep up as bystanders dodged the old man who seemed to be delivering a running overture of his dialogue to the overspill crowd in the hall.

"Then they were labeled by Lt. Gedney, as property, and salvage claimed on them, and under that process were taken into the custody of the marshal as property. Then they were claimed by Ruiz and Montez and again taken into custody by the court. The district Attorney of Connecticut wrote to the Secretary of State, stating –"

The bailiff called the court to order. "Oyez, Oyez, the court is in session, the honorable Judge Jenson presiding." The room was immediately quiet.

The judge slipped his glasses on, looked up from a letter, cleared his throat and tried to sound more judicial than angry. "To those concerned, you should hear this."

He read: "The Blacks who are indicted for the murder of the captain and mate, are now in jail in New Haven. The next term of our circuit court sits on the 17th, at which time I suppose, it will be my duty to bring them to trial, unless they are in some other way disposed of. I would respectfully inquire, sir, whether there are no treaty stipulations with the Government of Spain that would authorize our government to deliver them up to the Spanish authorities. This is the second intimation from the District Attorney. We shall find others. The Africans were fully in the custody of the Court. And he is anxious to know whether they cannot be disposed of in some way by the Executive, so that the courts of the United States may not be troubled to decide upon the case. God Bless America."

The judge looked up over his glasses from reading, paused and in a deeper tone pronounced, "Or so the president of the United States would have us believe."

Ingersoll stood placidly in the president's library trying to calm Van Buren who was pouring a large whisky into a small glass.

Van Buren slammed the crystal container down, blurting out: "Who the hell is president here!?"

One of the aides moved from the couch that all of a sudden seemed too close to the President's desk.

Ingersoll sat quietly, "Let's not react in desperation."

"Damn, damn, damn, desperation, everything is plowing up against us. We kicked Santa Ana's ass in '35 and now he's hoodooing the Mexicans again. Then the Mobile Alabama fire, hundreds of buildings burned. Now another Cherokee war. And wait, there's more. The price of cotton in New Orleans dropped fifty percent. Then—my banks are going broke—hell, they're all goin' broke."

"Well not completely broke sir." Ingersoll smiled over the rim of his tumbler. "This is the presidency." Hesitant, Van Buren looked for approval. Then with a forced laugh said. "I hope I didn't let you all down."

"No sir, you wrote a very succinct letter to the court, you got your points over, and now you, now you're—you've got it set right and move on. You're right where you oughta be."

The aide sat in a straight back chair, looked up from a stuffed folder in his lap and asked, "Do we have to be afraid of the supreme court?"

"Well, it's a difficult thing. For you, for John the rest, but Goddammit, I'm never going to discuss this son-of-a-bitching thing again."

The aide tied a string around his folder and smiled. "Yes sir. You've done it now. And you've laid out your position. You've taken your steps."

Ingersoll finished his whisky in one last gulp. "But let me say—you and all the rest, by God, keep the faith. You're going to win this…"

Van Buren put a cap on his bottle. "Absolutely."

Ingersoll got up to go find somewhere else for a much-needed refill. "You notice what I said to the press about violence and so forth on the other side."

"It's the damn wild-eyed Abolitionists".

Around the corner from the Bank Alley newspaper, published from a small print shop on Bank Alley, four newspapermen sat at the far end of the overflowing noisy bar flipping through their notes, double checking dates and names as they bantered caustically back and forth. The cartoonist Atkin sat next to the old reporter who had a white walrus mustache and wore a gauze hat that did a good job of covering his bald head. Three others wore long coats and leather knee-high boots. Two tall, another short, they looked like they lifted wagons for a living; the third one looked all of nineteen and was trying desperately to grow a mustache.

The barkeep was having trouble trying to keep track of who was saying what with their fast banter. Between the noise, the barmaid's drink orders, her wise ass retorts, and his constant sipping of beer, bartending was starting to get difficult. He squinted at the old reporter who was crossing out and rewriting and mumbling over his notes.

"June 1834, Speaker of the house Andrew Stevenson resigned from Congress to become Minister to the United Kingdom."

"Well, with Jackson's support. Polk ran for Speaker against fellow Tennessean John Bell and those damned Calhoun tags along, Richard Wilde, and Joel Sutherland," Atkin sniffed.

The short wagon lifter looked over at the near moustache and smiled, "That's spelled: S U T H E R L A N D, of Pennsylvania."

The young reporter nodded at everything said. "But, but that's all old news," he said hesitantly.

"No. It's called—background. You gotta know what causes shit," the short wagon lifter said. Then the tall and short lifters bantered back and forth.

"So, from 1833 to 34, it was Jackson who was engaged in removing federal funds from the Second Bank of the United States during the damn Bank war." Winking at the kid he added, "Thats more background."

"Ha. Sounds like at a penny a line, you got a lot of background there."

The bartender wiped beer foam from his mustache and interrupted, "Weren't it Calhoun who shot it down sayin' it was a dangerous grabbin' of power."

"He did something I'd never—"

"Called the men of the Jackson administration 'artful and cunning.'"

"Well maybe I'd a said corrupt and conniving politicians, and not fearless warriors."

"No-one could spend their worthless paper money."

"Land price bubble exploded."

"Bank's doors slammed shut or they just closed up and disappeared."

"And then, Van Buren got elected in '36."

"He got infected with Jackson's bank scheme, making the Panic of '37."

"Jackson infected lots."

"His parting speech?" short said.

"Ah yes, famous last words," the old writer said.

"I should have memorized it. It's a perfect example of hypocrisy," Short sighed. "Duplicity! But—I wrote it—somewhere—wait, wait—" Short flips through his notebook. "Ah, finally all the way at the last page of course. Here. And I quote Jackson: 'And is it supposed that the wandering savage has a stronger attachment to his home than the settled, civilized Christian? Is it more afflicting to him to leave the graves of his fathers than it is to our brothers and children?

Rightly considered, the policy of the General Government toward the red man is not only liberal, but generous. He is unwilling to submit to the laws of the States and mingle with their population. To save him from this alternative, or perhaps utter annihilation, the General Government kindly offers him a new home, and proposes to pay the whole expense of his removal and settlement."

The barmaid snorts, "Yeah, and ol' Davy Crockett blasted Jackson for violatin' the constitution and breakin' treaties, you know, for native American's land rights."

The kid looked at short-lifter then the barmaid.

"Too bad that damn Injun guide Junaluska saved Jackson at the battle of Horseshoe Bend," the barkeep snorted.

"The price of cotton went way South."

"Then the market crashed."

The kid scratched his near mustache. "I—Okay, okay, I get it." All three say in chorus, "Background."

"Bell said Jackson was ignorant on financial matters."

"Well he's half right," Old Timer said.

"Oh, I have a hard time believing Old Hickory doesn't know things," the nearly mustached the kid said.

"Kid you just buy the paper to read Charles Dickens serialized novels?" the tall wagon-lifter smirked.

"Ha, As evidence, he ..." The old reporter took a long swig of beer and tapped the top of the empty glass for a refill, wiping foam off his nose he continued, "Annnnd, he cited the economic panic caused by Nicholas Biddle—nine thousand banks went out of business overnight when the market crashed. "Damn Jefferson anti federal, bank radical, utopian, idealist hardhead—but cunning."

"Biddle, I met Biddle. Unworthy of making an impression, he is," Atkin said. "Hell, any man that loves cards, horse racing and gambling like ol' Hickory can't be all bad," Atkin laughed.

"Atkin? Stick to drawing your little Harper's cartoons, I'll write about the real world."

The old reporter rolled his eyes, pulled another battered pad out of a coat pocket, thumped through some notes and read. "On March 28, 1834, Calhoun voted with the Whig senators on a successful motion to censure Jackson for his removal of the funds. In 1837, he refused to attend the inauguration of Jackson's chosen successor, Van Buren, even as other powerful senators who opposed the administration, such as Webster and Clay, did witness the inauguration. However, by 1837 Calhoun generally had realigned himself with most of the Democrats' policies. But, there is that little thing called The Panic of 37." The old reporter took off his hat and ran his hand over the baldness and flipped several pages. "Now, the three African children that were brought in Court today, weeping, terrified at being separated."

"Heart-wrenching," said the young man.

"Well, the Marshal testified he was holding the African kids because Lt. Gedney claimed then as salvage."

"Can he do that?" mustache sounded surprised.

"Did."

"Kid, Armfield out of Alexandria houses his coffles in pens around Washington I wouldn't put a dog in."

"Coffles?"

The bartender sighed, shook and his head. "New slaves chained up in a line." "Oh."

"They don't need agent 355 to figure that." Barmaid said.

The nearly mustached looked up about to ask—The barmaid laughed and said before he had a chance to ask.

"Never heard of agent 355? Ha. Some newsmen. She was General Washington's secret agent in the revolution."

The old guy took a new beer, glanced out of the corner of his eye at his companions. "Then the Court heard for Montez's tergiversation. Changing his mind this a way and that a way."

The young reporter looked up surprised, "Tergiv...? good, that's good."

"So much better than betrayal," the tall writer nodded.

"Can you spell that? Ah, then Mr. Sedgewick read his statement for the Africans..." The young man said, looking up from his scribbling into the bartender's eyes that bounced back and forth like a metronome looking between the fast-talking writers.

"... then Mr. Baldwin argued that the court did not have jurisdiction as the ship was found at Long Island, in the district of New York."

"It's like a bloody chess game," Atkin added quickly as one of the regular bar flies almost sat in his lap while hefting himself up on a stool.

"Wait... wait. then, he argued Gedney had no rights as salvor, Montez illegally imported the slaves—and— the American district Attorney was not authorized to make any claim on behalf of the Spanish Government in America."

"Then the Grand Jury came in and asked the court to give them instructions regarding the murder—alleged murder—on board the Amistad."

"Alleged? What'd the judge say?" Mustache asked over the barroom noise as a group of laughing teamsters burst in.

"The offense of Cinque and his associates?"

"Associates?" Barfly held up one finger.

"Self-protection's some offense," the bartender managed to slip in as he pulled an ale for barfly.

"Well, he said it took place on board a Spanish vessel at sea, so, it didn't have any validity in our courts."

"That won't make Van Buren happy!" said Barfly, trying to focus on Atkin.

"A weak president," Atkin sniffed.

"Be nice now, he's the son of a tavern owner," the barman smirked.

"But a strong pro-slaver," the old reporter nodded.

"Hell, George Washington owned slaves when he was president."

"John Adams didn't," Mustache added.

"Jefferson did," the bartender added quickly.

"Well, he got rid of the government corruption," Atkin said.

"Dirty government, dirty government," Mustache laughed.

"You still talking about his slaves," the barmaid said as she wiggled by.

"He removed a lot a politicians that he felt were crooked," Atkin suggested.

"Don't change the subject," the old guy barked.

"He rewarded the faithful with an office," the old barfly burped.

"He had slaves dammit—you think he cares about Amistad?" the bartender snapped.

"Who?" Barfly asked.

"Well Van Buren sure don't care," Atkin nodded.

"Madison either." The barmaid returned.

"Monroe too," Atkin sighed.

"Me too," quipped Barfly.

"Well hell, seven out of nine U.S. Supreme Court justices are southern slave-owners," the old writer insisted.

"Well John Quincy Adams never ever," Atkin replied.

"Ol' Hickory did, and while he's president." Atkin tried to focus but lost who was in the conversation. The barmaid smiled and filled his glass.

"Van Buren got rid of his before he got the presidency."

"He sure don't sound like it."

"He doesn't want this case in court?" the kid asked.

"What gave you the clue?"

After long years of experience, the barkeep never changed expression, just looked from reporter to reporter, and wiped the bar. The reporters wrote, crossed out, and rewrote furiously over their beers, and kept talking at a rapid-fire pace, and ogling the busty barmaid who showed them more than a little flesh as she bent to hit the tap and pull more beer. She looked up, smiled and said, "You fellas best remember, it was a pro-slavery mob that shot an' killed that poor reporter, what's his name, Lovejoy—in Alton Illinois wasn't it?"

CHAPTER THIRTEEN

It started to rain as the young reporter with nearly a mustache grabbed two papers from a kid on the corner hawking the news. He stuffed them in his coat pocket and hurried two blocks to the Bird and Bottle Inn. There was an overflow crowd from the courtroom having lunch and a drink. He planned to interview them while waiting for the trial to start up again. Several dozen were students, about half were businessmen, some rich, had some poor; the rest were "Americans" who nobody could really understand. They were an assortment of Southern, Spanish, Italian, French, Irish, Scots, and German/American accents and had an impossible time understanding each other's politics or pronunciations.

All were very vocal. Many who hadn't been able get in the packed court kept interrupting various political conversations and loudly debated back and forth in the four connected main rooms and garden. Barmaids rushed in and out of the crowd with pitchers of ale and beer. One of the college students from Georgetown had a bouncing Jack: a dancing Black puppet, with hinged arms and legs that clickety clacked on a paddle. He kept it dancing—to the annoyance of several patrons and the delight of his friends.

The mustached kid pushed past a bunch of students, stood on a chair, pulled a newspaper out of his coat pocket, and read as loud as a town crier over the fast banter of his audience. Yelling over the clatter of the crowd, kitchen, and street noises he broadcast yesterday's news. "First, since none of you seem to know your history, a little background: In 1444 the first public sale of African slaves in Lagos, Portugal. In 1482 Portugal built the first auction house for slaves in Ghana. The first slave ship arrives in South America in 1510."

He paused to grab a mug from a barmaid rushing by. "1518 the first shipload got here from Africa. 1777— And—Huzza! Let's hear it for Vermont! the first state here to abolish slavery. 1792—Denmark banned slavery in its colonies. 1807—Britain outlawed their slave trade. 1811—Spain abolished legal trading of slaves—on paper. Sweden banned slaving in 1813, then the Netherlands banned slaving in 1814. 1819—Portugal abolishes slave trade—north of the equator. Finally, France banned it 1826. 1833! Britain passed slave Abolition Act. Okay. Now, a little background for today's headlines."

One of the barflies shouts, "Either get to the murders and rape, or sit down and have a beer." But undaunted, mustache plows on.

"Wait, wait, more background. Calhoun's father, Patrick Calhoun, a staunch supporter of slavery, taught his son that social standing depends not merely on a commitment to the ideal of popular self-government but also on the ownership of a substantial number of slaves. Flourishing in a world in which slaveholding was a hallmark of civilization, Calhoun saw little reason to question its morality as an adult."

An old drunk squints at Mustache and burps out, "Kid you pimpin' for Calhoun?"

A jovial group in back thought that was funny. Mustached turned his volume up. "He further believed that slavery instilled in the remaining whites a code of honor that blunted the disruptive potential of private gain and fostered the civic mindedness that lay near the core of the republican creed. From such a standpoint, the expansion of slavery decreased the likelihood for social conflict and postponed the declension when money would become the only measure of self-worth, as had happened in New England."

Barfly shouted, "God please, someone buy him a beer, he can't talk and drink."

Mustache continued "Calhoun asserted that slavery was a 'positive good.' He rooted this claim on two grounds: 'white supremacy and paternalism.' Enough background! Now, as you may know, Mr. Cleveland delivered on behalf of the house of Montez of Havana, who were on the Amistad." Mustache read even louder from his notes, "We deny any right of salvage to Lt. Gedney and others. Being in the service and pay of the United States, they were bound to render assistance without compensation. Capt. Green, having not in fact saved the vessel and cargo, is not entitled to salvage, as that should be given for saving—not for the attempt to save." The crowd was split, some of the young listened, the older crowd turned to the bar and started their own loud evaluations.

Mustached banged the wall. "Hey! I'm reporting here!" He continued even louder. "Rodger Baldwin's cornerstone of defense argued that fraudulent documents could not make free men slaves, being an outright violation of Spain's own anti-slavery laws."

With a heavy Irish brogue and drinking straight from a pitcher, a heavy dock worker bellows, "Ey da Spaniards argues da goods on board belong ta Spain an da Blacks 're goods—"

One of the William and Marry students laughs, "Well, Adams did say it's dangerous times when you're afraid to turn your back on your own goods."

A Georgian accent adds, "And they should be returned to Havana to stand trial for killing Cubans."

Mustache steps down shaking his head. "I give up."

"Give me liberty or give me Cuba," a very Yale voice chortles.

"Was that Patrick Henry?"

The Georgian stands, "So what would you have done?"

The Bostonian's friend chimes in, "What would Thomas Paine have done?"

"Great example! A jailbird didn't have the common sense of a yeller dog."

Ready to try again, having grabbed another beer and jumped back on a table, the nearly Mustached reporter looks down at the Georgian accent. "Newspapers North and South are carryin' the Amistad story." He pulls out another paper, unfolds it dramatically, and starts reading. "The suspicious looking schooner was captured and brought into port! Much excitement had been created in New York for the past week, from the reports of several pilot boats having seen and been fired upon by a clipper-built schooner off the Hook, full of..." He points at friends in the group like a conductor. "Fill in your favorite politically correct adjectives!"

All stopped, smiled, and raised their glasses.

Georgian: "Cannibals."

"Pirates," the barkeep said as he hustled through the crowd to the bar.

Georgian's friend bellowed, "Nigrahs!"

"Blacks."

"Africans."

"Savages," is hard to understand with a boozy Portuguese accent.

"Captives."

"Kidnapped Africans."

"Freedom fighters," came in unison from four students holding each other up. Mustache tossed his empty glass and grabbed someone's beer off the table and drank deeply, inhaled and read from another paper. "Ingersoll said, and I quote: The Court should not interfere by a summary process—depriving his clients of the opportunity of establishing their rights as owners. Whatever that means."

"They should hang 'em as pirates."

"They were freemen in Africa."

"The United States got no right to go beyond the Spanish papers."

"Treaty says, any property should be returned to the owners."

"It's the law!?"

"Spaniards got law too," a woman at the bar bellowed.

"Hmph. This ain't Spain," added her husband.

The band strikes up after taking a beer break.

A sailor in canvas whites added over the loud band of banjos, "If a British cruiser had a found 'em they would have set 'em free."

"An' got five guineas a head for it," laughed the bartender.

"Lieutenant Gedney'll gets his salvage money from the slavers," said with a French accent, lost in the crowd, after downing a tumbler of rum.

"They's Cubans what's the south got a bug up their ass about?"

"Hell, southern state's got laws."

"Ha. Most got outlaws."

"States' rights."

"You mean states' wrongs."

"He sounds like one of them nullifiers: Any state has a right to nullify such laws of the United States as might not be acceptable to them."

"You gotta pay four different taxes haulin' goods from Maine ta New Jersey. That's your damn states' rights."

"Washington doesn't know what states need. Only the states know."

"Then what's your congressman doing in Washington! He's from your state ain't he? Course, he don't know nothing".

A tall lanky red headed Yale student who looked all of fourteen shoute, "So your congressman ain't doin' his job. Fire 'm!"

His buddy in a Yale sweater leaned over, pointed, and cackled, "It's your congressman, you voted for him."

His friend adds, "If you're both ever *in* your state."

Mustache couldn't pass up saying, "Is that the state of confusion?"

The red headed student crowed, "Probably folks voted for him just to get him out o' th' state." The three students laughed and clicked their mugs together.

"Everybody's got their own laws. You can't dip a toe across a border without getting a tariff or arrested for doing what's illegal over here, that ain't legal ten foot over there. Ain't no rights at all I sez. States' rights is un-American."

Mustache added, "States rights means slavery."

The voice from Georgia blurted out, "You think your state can stop my state from importin' slaves?"

"Congress can't tell Mississippians how to think."

"They can't tell a turnip how to think either. Same thing," Red said and raised his drink to his three friends who all clicked glasses.

"Who can tell if congress thinks at all?"

"Hey! Can Mississippians think?"

The owner and a barkeep nervously stepped between the two groups and filled mugs.

"Order comes from thought!" blurted out one of the three.

Red mocked, "Ah, Kant. Knowledge by the inherent nature of the mind."

Nearly Mustached chuckled, "It don't matter what the hell happens, question is does it feel good."

"Some call that the Categorical Imperative," Red nods.

"Or thinking without knowledge."

"Or knowledge without thinking."

"Are you certain of that? Really certain?" Red said and broke out laughing.

"Ah, Descartes. Are you sure?" Mustache said with a serious face.

"A bunch of lil' states fightin' against each other." Growled a Georgian unhappy with the sophomoric intellectual mocking of the students.

"It's a foreign plot!" An old Scotsman blurted out. Four Southern students were ready to swat the pesky mosquito-like students who reveled in being bad boys.

Red looked down at the old five-foot short Scotsman. "Divide and conquer! It worked for Julius."

The debate was getting louder and more heated with each gulp of ale. Most of the students were tipsy and just having fun. However, several customers were about to explode. Shouting back and forth got confusing. Even those who were just eating lost track of who said what and why.

Short Scot puffed-up to Red, reached up and poked him in the chest. "I fought and my brother died at Concord, for the right of free men to govern ourselves. And I'll fight again."

Red stopped laughing. "Freedom to make slaves? Freedom to take someone else's freedom?"

Short Scot stretched up on his toes and managed to eyeball Red's Adam apple. "No one got the right to tell me how—"

"Well, you ain't a slave are ya," Red said.

"Na now! But I wa' indentured by a bleedin' Scots landlord an' shipped here when I was but 9."

"You do look somewhat African." One of the young Yale-ies said just before he got pushed hard in the belt. "Heyyyy!"

Three barmen jumped in between the Scot and the student as several patrons started swinging at each other. Another barkeep grabbed the student, and the bar owner and a student grabbed the Scotsman and ran him out the door.

"Shut it, ya scabby naff dobber! Let me go! Let me at em! Fatherless pups, it's a sad day they outlawed the dueling."

The owner slammed the door. "That's enough of that!" Then from the main room came more cursing.

"Hell, what happened to: together we stand divided we fall."

"Them Niggrah's killed three white men."

"Then who's responsible for the sixteen Africans that died on the ship?"

"Then Montez is a murderer too?"

"Well the captain killed em, an he's dead."

The short rebel growled, "They was merchandise. Property plain an simple."

"The rights of the owners are guaranteed," Georgia shouts, ducking back from the doorway when the barkeep points and scowls at him.

"Ergo... the President is bound to surrender them," his friend shouted.

"What about the rights of the Africans?"

"Slaves got no rights," Georgia shouts in and ducks out of the doorway again as the barkeep stomps back in his direction.

"They were free in Africa."

"Well they shoulda stayed in Africa."

Glascock of Georgia had been watching in the crowd, and he can't take any more of the Yankee student's flippant attitude. With the fervor of a Southern Baptist minister, he banged his half-full mug on the table and bellowed. "It were on November seventh, a mob attack on the Alton, Illinois newspaper editor Elijah Lovejoy. Lovejoy was killed, because of his anti-slavery writings. Several persons were indicted in the killing but found not guilty.

"Lovejoy was killed while defending a newly arrived printing press. People opposed to Lovejoy's opinion had already destroyed three previous presses. Damnation! The truth? The truth is that man as property has existed in all ages of the world, and results from the natural state of man—which is war.

"When God created the first family and gave them the fields of the earth as an inheritance, one of the numbers, in obedience to the impulses and passions that had been implanted in the human heart, rose and slew his brother. This universal nature of man is alone modified by civilization and law. War, conquest, and force, have produced slavery, and it is a state necessary to the internal law of self-preservation, that will ever perpetuate and defend it."

Glascock's outbreak was so vehement that the room was quiet for a beat.

"Achh! Damn old Adams can leck mich am arsch! Tearing dis' country apart."

The quiet German sitting by the door got up and doffed his hat, "Vhat you think vill habben vhen two million Schwarze—dey go rampaging after dey hear dis? Mine Gott vhat folly!" He pushed his way out, mumbling, "Geh zum Teufel."

At the sound of the clock chiming, the barkeep shouted "Two o'clock! Court's back in session."

The group—barely kept from fighting, gulped their ale, and ran for the door. The streets were loud with horse and buggy traffic as people flooded the pavement to the courthouse. The Bird & Bottle was empty.

CHAPTER FIFTEEN

February 24th, 1841

Like a swarm of wasps, the crowd pushed into the courtroom. The courtroom marshal pointed his billy club at six rowdy students. There was murmured confusion as everyone settled in and tried to hear the bailiff as Cinque was sworn in. Then, with a glare at the audience from the judge the trial started. James Covey translated.

The humidity was so heavy it would have been almost as easy to wade through the Lomboko river than walk through the sweltering air. Loading at the slave depot merged groups of Africans chained in long lines. The captives were marched to the docks in front of the fort on well-used trails. Cannons stuck out of the parapets around the thick, forty-foot-high walls. Black armed guards patrolled all around. Several long docks led out into the river delta. The limp Spanish flag barely stirred over the fort in the lifeless air.

Herded through heavy wooden gates into the confusion of the stark gray courtyard, several hundred Africans were divided up, assigned to their 'owners' ships, and chained head, hand, and foot. A blacksmith would fix a heavy black iron collar around the neck of each slave.

The collars were two semi-circle arms hinged in back with a hole in each arm of the other side. The chain was run through the holes pinched tight around the slave's neck, locked, and four feet of chain attached to the next slave's collar. A lock at the end of the chain was fixed to an iron loop in a wall or post. As many as twenty slaves or more could be on one chain. Tragically, if a British man of war came upon a slaver, the slave ship's captain would order slaves, who were attached to each other, thrown overboard. And ask the British "What slaves?"

A black guard counted the number of slaves on his manifest. A guard pulled the group toward the blacksmiths. He stopped the slave line and told two blacksmiths to separate the chain at Bau. Bau's chain was cut three feet in front of him. Bau, his wife, and child were separated.

Bau cried out and his wife tried to run to him with their child but her chains caught against the next slaves, tearing at the flesh on her neck. She was hit across the face with the butt of a whip by one of the African guards. Bau is kicked between the legs and dragged from the blacksmiths. Bau's wife and child are marched down to one of the piers. A dozen boats of various flags loaded eight different lines of chains of slaves that day. The white captains and crew went about their business as if stacks of wood were being loaded. Paddling around the river bend a dozen Africans in a long canoe sang a rowing song. Seeing the ships, they stopped singing.

Several Black guards on the ship pointed the way to the slave hold. The chains of African slaves rattled against the iron hatch opening as they descended, casting long shadows from the late sun on the deck, then disappeared into the blackness below. "On board the vessel, from

Africa, there was a large number of men, but the women and children were far the most numerous. We were fastened together in couples by the wrists and legs and kept in chain day and night."

Bau's wife was pulled into the three-foot high slave deck. The slaves were squished side by side. Bau's wife cried out in pain as the chains dragged against her flesh. The baby cried louder.

The voice of Covey flowed around the courtroom as he translated Cinque's testimony. "There was only 3 feet 4 inches from the floor to the ceiling of the boat. It was impossible to stand upright for all except the children. We were given just enough rice to eat, but not much to drink. If anyone was sick and could not eat, they were beaten. So they ate and vomited. Many men, women, and children died on the passage." Covey stopped for a moment to regain his composure, he glared at Ruiz, then continued. "They landed by night at a small village near Havana. They, we, were shackled and marched through the town to bins and were able to sleep outdoors in the warm breezes of the island. It was the first night of real sleep. White men came to buy us. One of the men was Ruiz."

Cinque sat down, the court officer stood, "The court calls Mr. D. Francis Bacon as witness for the defense." Dr. Bacon took the oath and was asked what he knew about the holding pens for the slaves.

"I know the place called Dumbokoro by the Spaniards. It is an island in the river Gallinas. There is a large slave depot there. It is said to belong to the house of Martinez in Havana; there are different establishments on the island. I saw American, Russian, Spanish, and Portuguese flagged vessels there. The American flag is a complete shelter; no

British man-of-war would dare to capture an American vessel. The slave trade on that part of the coast is the business of the country. Africans make war all over Africa, just to take slaves. Towns and villages make war just for slaves. Some are sold because of crimes, some for debts of course. Many slaves stay in Africa. Most slaves are brought to the coast for sale, as no white man dare penetrate the inlands."

Dr. Madden was an Irish doctor and writer. Her Majesty's Commissioner of Inquiry for British Settlements. An avid abolitionist and historian, he took an active role in advocating anti-slavery rules in the Caribbean. The Marshal ushered Doctor Robert Madden in and introduced him to the court.

The bailiff introduced Doctor Madden, whose first encounter with slavery was in the Middle East in the Ottoman Empire, which found him in what would become his first in a dangerous series of human rights missions. Born in Dublin, he established a thriving medical practice in London. He abandoned his career as a fashionable Mayfair physician and devoted full-time to the anti-slavery cause.

"Your honor, Robert Madden to be sworn in. Member of the Anti-Slavery Commission in Havana. His deposition for the Africans, as to the prisoners being newly captured from Africa." The bailiff asked Madden, "To tell the whole truth so help you God."

" — So help me God."

The lawyer asked, "Dr Madden, please tell us your background and interest in this case."

"I am a British subject and have been a resident at Havana for more than three years, I had official stations there for three years. My office is Commissioner of Liberated Africans, and The British Commissioner of the Mixed Court of Justice. These duties made me well acquainted with the details of slavery and the slave trade in Cuba.

"The Cuba of 1839 was a much crowded island since de Ocampo first put a Spanish foot on it. After that buccaneers, pirates and French Corsairs roamed its shores freely. Those days the Havana streets smelled of sugar cane wagons that bumped through the crowded city from the new railroad station that ran from Bejucal to the mill. Wagon loads of barrels of molasses went to a distillery, and barrels of rum came out of the distillery to the docks. Fishing fleets also unloaded at these docks.

"Havana grew with trade to the French, Spanish, and Great Britain. Wealth was flourishing in Havana. Construction of cultural facilities like the Tacon Theatre, one of the most luxurious theaters in the world, the Artistic and Literary Liceo, and the theater Coliseo were built mostly by slave labor. And slavery was big business. The fact that slavery was legal in Cuba led to the American South's investment there.

"Havana and its slave market was one of the three most active ports in all of Latin America. Trade with the European continent poured in through the port. Spain built the fort to be the strongest in Latin America and organized flotillas of ships that were protected by Spanish armadas against pirates and privateers.

"Wealthy Havana merchants could watch chain line after chain line of new slaves marched from ships to the auction block. As many as ten slave lines at a time wound their way to the slave market from the docks through active street markets. Locals would maybe pause a second, then they continued on as if unaffected by the sight of beaten-down slaves slogging through the streets otherwise filled with the happy sounds of children playing and music from overcrowded bars."

One of those slaves was Bau who anxiously scanned the other chains of slaves looking for his wife. Another slave, Cinque, stooped quickly, picked up a bent nail on the dock where crates were being opened. He slipped it into his armpit and walked on. Two Black slaves, cracking open crates watched, smiled knowingly, and continued their unloading.

"I had written report after report on Cuban auctions where slaves were held bunched together in large pens like cattle. Carriages of rich families arrived in parades with baskets of food and wine for the viewing of the slaves. Indigo and sugar cane planters lost several hundred slaves each harvest season, slashing with machetes hour after hour in humid ninety-five-degree weather. Slave holders said it was a natural climate for their African slaves. But they died. Doctor Madden wrote that a field of fifteen— to twenty-foot-tall cane with cutting sharp leaves was dangerous all by itself.

"Rapid cutting and processing of cane required 18 to 20-hour days. Slaves worked on millions of acres of sugar cane plantations. Nearly half the farmland in Cuba was planted in sugar cane. Slaves labored in sugar mills were subject to terrible conditions, rigorous manual labor beginning at the early age of nine or ten with sunup to sun down days during harvest. Processing included cultivating, cutting crops, hauling wagons, and processing sugarcane.

"Slaves were crowded into locked cages that were swarming with fleas and ticks, rarely getting more than four hours sleep. In the sweltering tropical heat conditions were harsh, unsanitary, humid and extremely hot. There was little if any ventilation in the holding pens, where windows were small, barred, and little more than a hole in the wall. Prior to the auctions, Spanish officers counted the slaves as they entered. New slaves in chains were herded past more slaves on the auction blocks.

The rich gathered, the women socialized, the men talked trade and examined slaves as wine, coffee, and hors d'ourves were served with sweets by liveried Blacks. Other buyers lounged in an elaborate canopied arcade while a Black band on the lawn played for the guests. Back in the holding pens blacksmiths removed chains. Guards laughed at the naked African men and women huddled in stalls. I've seen buckets of water thrown on them to wash them down and a trough of gruel dumped in each pen."

Hesitantly Grabeau looked around the huge courtroom at all the people in their Sunday best. Covey interpreted and began to speak faster and faster as Grabeau remembered the trials and pain they suffered through, "Ruiz made them stand in a row. He then felt each of them in every part of the body. He made them open their mouth, and then bend over. He patted us down like a horse dealer. We were taken on foot through Havana by Ruiz and men at night. We were put in irons. We were very, very hungry and suffered much in the hot days and nights from thirst. In addition to this there was much whipping. The cook laughed and told us that when we reached the plantation, we would all be eaten. This made our hearts burn. To avoid being eaten and escape the bad treatment we rose against the crew and took the ship to return to Africa."

As the performer he was, Madden turned dramatically and addressed the audience. "In the last three years there were over twenty-three thousand slaves, that we know of, from Africa, introduced yearly into Cuba although that was in violation of Spanish law ever since 1820. All told we believe there has been more than 800,000 slaves imported to Cuba—twice as many as those shipped to the southern states of America. The Spanish authorities never interfere but connive at it — receiving ten dollars a head for every Negro they pass. They call this a voluntary contribution, but in reality it is a tax, an illegal tax. I have seen the Africans who were captured aboard the Amistad, they are of that class called in Cuba, Bozal, a term given to Negroes recently from Africa.

"Customarily Negroes illegally introduced by slave traders to the Havana, are taken immediately to the Barracoons, or slave marts, which are fitted up exclusively for the reception and sale of Bozal Negroes. They are kept by traders for no more than three weeks, fattened up like farm animals, then sold. The most openly notorious of the slavers is Martinez and Co. Here trespasses, or permits, are given simply on application by Martinez to the authorities. No oath is required—just payment of fees. The Bozal negroes are now called Ladinos, and given papers to be traded."

When he arrived in Cuba, dazed, Bau saw his wife holding a dead baby three pens away. Chained and beaten, there was nothing he could do. One of the black guards saw this and motioned to another guard. The baby was forced from the mother, who wouldn't admit the infant was dead. The guard put the body on a cart of bodies pulled by a slave. Children over eight were separated from their mothers and put in a pen together. As Bau was marched in with his group he searched the line of women being led to the stocks. Bau's wife, barely able to focus, looked directly at him but didn't recognize him.

Sedgewick stood and faced the judge, "Your Honor! The Blacks of the Amistad knew nothing of Cuba, or the Spanish language. These Africans were born free, are entitled to their freedom; every person is presumed to be a freeman until the contrary is proved."

Hollabird quickly added, "Relating to the case as brought by the Spanish counsel, there is no law in force in Cuba prohibiting the importation of slaves from Africa ... and the court of mixed commission at Havana has jurisdiction over cases of only those slaves captured at sea."

Sedgewick scowled at Hollabird. "The Libelists and the United States claim they were slaves, because licenses have been produced authorizing the transportation of ladinos from one port in Cuba to another, a term totally inapplicable to the Amistad captives."

Adams suffered from rheumatism in his hands, his eyes were sensitive to light, a problem John Adams senior also had. He would tear up as if crying, not an image to present before the court. For the last twenty years he had worried about going blind. The pain was sometimes so intense he couldn't sleep. His eyes would swell and stick together feeling, he said, as if four hooks were pulling his eye apart. A doctor attached leeches to his eye to take the swelling down, but the pain persisted. He sat with a white cloth to his eye, straining to listen and see Sedgewick speak as Covey translated quietly to Cinque.

Sedgewick stood. "It is perfectly evident from the licenses that a fraud has been committed upon, or worse, *by* the Spanish authorities. The decree of Spain of 1817 prohibits the slave trade after 1820, with heavy penalties, and declares all slaves imported from Africa, after that period, be freed."

Lawyer Isham, for the Navy officers, stood. "On behalf of Lt. Gedney and Meade, I must take occasion to say, that my clients authorize me to say—they would never receive salvage on human flesh. All they ask for is *that if* the Court decides that the vessel, cargo, and slaves, should be restored to the Spaniards, it should be upon terms that the owners should first pay them a reasonable compensation for services rendered in preserving their property."

One of the students pokes his buddy on the arm and guffaws, "Ha. They want a be sort of pregnant?!"

Pandemonium broke out in the courtroom. The Yale students' laughter covered Judge Judson banging his gavel. He gave up. Green stood and shouted, "How can men on an American ship of war ask salvage for doing their duty?"

Full of gossip and a few brews the pub regulars quieted down as Adams and his entourage entered. But the crowds' own interpretations of the day was too much to keep quiet and they all returned to their gossip and drinks. Adams ordered a glass of hard cider and sat at the end of a table with six others. He was holding a damp cloth to his left eye. James arrived, hurried through the pub, and leaned close Adams' shoulder, distracting him with news. The other aides continued talking, eyeing them, trying to figure what's being said, but keeping their conversation low. The rest of the room gossiped on for anyone to hear.

"The judge?

"He's a dyed-in-the-wool Jackson man."

"Adams lost his second term to Jackson."

"Only the dirtiest presidential fight ever."

Another aide rushed in, bumped into James, and wide-eyed whispered to Adams, "Thornton told me to tell you Mr. Webster wishes to see you. He said a member of the

Senate of Massachusetts had written to him concerning the Northeastern Boundary question."

Adams exhales, "Oh, Christ, not enough to worry about."

Adams patted the white cotton cloth against his eye, drank deeply, and handed his glass to the young barmaid who asked if she could get him a little piece of ice from the ice cellar, he held up a hand to thank her. She hurried off with the young aides watching her.

"It's the damn left eye," he sighed "threatening me with complete disability to perform my final duty before the Supreme Court. Anyhow, ahh, of the Supreme Court Justices, only two seem likely to favor the Africans: Story of Massachusetts, and Thompson of New York. All the others have been appointed by President Jackson, who, of course, is a Southern slave holder."

"And a bitter political enemy."

Adams nodded. "President Van Buren was a Jackson appointee; McLean is a political animal and two-faced. Baldwin's eccentric at best. Barbour's a shallow-pated wildcat. More of Georgia is a slave holder, Tennessee's, Catron is a Jackson man. Don't ever get in a poker game with that bunch. Too many signals going back and forth. Argh, Congress becomes more and more like Augean's stable."

James stared blankly at Adams without asking the question. Adams smiled and looked at James with his right eye. "From the tasks of Hercules. Augeas the king of Elis, of the Peloponnesus, had a stable full of three thousand immortal cattle that produced a monumental amount of manure—and, very much like Congress, hadn't been cleaned out in thirty years. So, it seems the gods made the cleaning of that stable Hercules fifth task. For the fabled Hercules, it was easy. He just diverted a river."

James laughed, "Aha. That's why you swim in the Potomac every day."

Meanwhile the Grampus was taking on supplies in New Haven Harbor.

February 24th, 184

The same crowd pushed up into the back of the courtroom and down to the main gallery. Above the judge, past the courtroom's American flag, the morning light flared off the golden eagle on the courtroom wall. After the familiar opening dialogue of the Bailiff and the Judge, John Quincy Adams stood, holding a white handkerchief in his left hand.

He started slowly, almost cautiously and built, "The indignation of the freemen of Connecticut, ought not tamely endure the sight, of thirty-six free persons, though Africans, fettered and manacled in their land of freedom. Then transported beyond the seas, to perpetual servitude or to death by the American President to please a foreign minister. The Spanish Minister files his petition on the grounds of the treaty of 1795: relying on the law of nations. This is so peculiar I can't even think of its application. The minister says that if permitted to pass unpunished, this would endanger the internal tranquility and safety of the island of Cuba, where citizens of the US carry on trade and own land which they cultivate with slave labor.

"They say these slaves, learning of the Amistad, would revolt. To guard against this would be a great expense. The Spanish minister has no right to appeal to our courts to pass sentence in consideration for their interest, or of American citizens that are subject to the laws of Spain. Calderon de la Barca refers to the treaty of 1795, articles

8 and 9 to support his demands. So. By the treaty of 1795: 'If persons, whether in public and of war, or private and of merchants, be forced to harbor or retreat into any rivers, bays, roads or ports with all humanity—they shall enjoy all favor, protection, and help at reasonable rates.' Gentlemen, this is an article for those in distress! Who was the Spanish owner here with his ship? There was none. I say the Africans are here in their ship."

The courtroom erupted. The state objected. The Judge banged his gavel. Adams, true to form, turned to face the room and smiled at the brouhaha he had inspired.

"If you say the original owner is referred to, in whose name was the ship's register given? He is dead and cannot claim benefit of this article. It is now an African vessel. And yet they did not bring the vessel into our waters. Truth is they were deceived, against their will, by the two Spaniards." Adams gestured to Ruiz and Montez.

"Now, if this court should consider this voyage from Lomboko, in Africa, was a violation of the laws of the United States, then the Spaniards are responsible for that offense. But suppose article 8 is applicable; what is the United States to do? They must place the Africans in possession, with the two Spaniards as their prisoners, to continue their voyage, which on their part was certainly lawful. Article 9? All ships and merchandise shall be rescued out of the hands of any pirates or robbers on the high seas and *shall be rendered up entire.*

"Who were the pirates and robbers? Were they the Africans? But they were brought from Lomboko, against the laws of Spain, against the laws of the United States and all nations. And rendered up entire? Does that mean that we must give up sixteen Americans for the sixteen who died as merchandise. Does this court define merchandise as human? Or humans as merchandise? But your honors, what, in your opinion was the duty of the Secretary of State? And what did he do? His first act was to misrepresent the demand and write to the District Attorney in Connecticut, directing him to demand the Africans as Spanish property. And ordered that no court should place them beyond the control of the President. And stated, that if the court should find they were not slaves by the laws of Spain, but that they were brought to our shores in violation of the act of Congress suppressing the slave trade, they should be placed at the disposal of the President. Those instructions do not appear here. Why? It was for information not incompatible with the public interest, that that proviso was kept back. I know of these things.

CHAPTER SIXTEEN

It had been a quiet Irish pub until it was filled full of Yale that afternoon. A much welcome break had been offered for the law students to go to the "Pirates" trial. The songs were ongoing and merrily sung by the incoming students who having been years in training at this establishment all knew the ditty at play. The Banjo player set the pace and the singing started. After the first beer was pulled by a tenor raising his mug high, he started an old favorite. "As I went home on Wednesday night as drunk as drunk could be," The chorus was quickly joined in by all.

The barmaid goosed the tenor as she skirted by and winked. Professor Hitchcock held up his watch and pointed at the door. The group was in full throat and not about to stop their caroling. Some could even hold a note, but they all knew the lyrics.

The day is clear and brisk. Hitchcock and Daggett, professors of law, Dr. Tully, and Rev. Taylor lead the crowd of law students from Philadelphia, New York, Wilkes Co NC. Page Co Va., Augusta, Montgomery, Syracuse, Chicago, and Hillsboro. At least thirty Northern and Southern students, in good voice, were dismissed from classes at Yale to attend the trial. A couple headed for another bar on the way shouting mean but humorous insults at the group who continued singing the fast-paced Irish ditty all the way to the courthouse. Two harmonicas in lockstep with the banjo player who led the march increasing the beat with each new stanza. They wound their way through the traffic and the laughter of the pedestrians, who hustled out of their way. Still in good voice the Yale lads snaked through the crowded streets singing:

> "As I went home on Thursday night as drunk as
> drunk could be
> I saw two boots beneath the bed where my old
> boots should be.
> Well, I called me wife and I said to her: Will
> you answer to me,
> Who owns them boots beneath the bed where
> my old boots should be?
> Ah, you're drunk, you're drunk you silly old
> fool, still you can not see?
> They're two lovely Geranium pots me mother
> sent to me.
> Well, it's many a day I've travelled a hundred
> miles or more
> But laces in Geranium pots I never saw before.
> As I went home on Saturday night as drunk as
> drunk could be
> I saw two hands upon her breasts where my old
> hands should be.
> Well, I called me wife and I said to her: Will
> you kindly answer me
> Who owns them hands upon your breasts
> where my old hands should be?

Ah, you're drunk, you're drunk you silly old
fool, still you can not see?
That's a lovely night gown that me mother sent
to me.
Well, it's many a day I've travelled a hundred
miles or more
But fingers in a night gown sure I never saw
before."

The singers made their way through the crowded
street past an amused group of sailors and a disapproving
group of mothers who hurried their children out of the
way. The kids would never know what the last verse was
because the singers arrived at the courthouse with a long
last banjo riff and joined the crowd. Several uniformed
officers pointed threateningly at them. The general hubbub
of the gathering had the energy of betters in line at a horse
track figuring the odds of who was going to win place
and show. There was standing room only. The courtroom
was so full of their own opinions Buddha, Moses, Jesus,
and Joseph Smith would have had trouble converting
them. It took Judge Judson several minutes pummeling
his podium's desktop to quiet the courtroom chatter. But
the courthouse marshal maladroitly tried to control the
crowd. An aide closed the two large open windows—barely
reducing the street noise.

The marshal cleared his throat and announced, "Order,
order, all be seated. You. Down. Judge Judson presiding.
Order I say. Madam please… sit, stay." The audience settled.
Hollabird walked forward as Antonio jauntily took the
chair. The judge glared at four latecomers. District Attorney
Hollabird postured dramatically and opened with Antonio's

testimony. The spectators forgot for the moment that he was owned, a slave of the Spaniards. He had testified that the Africans were well treated with plenty of food. Cinque killed the Captain, and would have killed him too.

Covey translated to Cinque. At the mention of Cinque's name the court turned to where he and a dozen other of the Amistad's Blacks sat huddled together with blankets wrapped around their shoulders.

Hollabird dramatically strode forward gesticulating. "If Senor Ruiz and Senor Montez have been engaged in illegal slave traffic, it is the duty of the United States government to return the Africans to the Spanish authorities in order that justice may be obtained. But that is not the province of this court. The Africans should be held for such action as the United States Government may feel proper. This is a problem of international diplomacy to be handled only by the President of the United States."

Before Covey can finish translating to the Africans, Hollabird turned and pointed at Cinque. "Who killed the captain! Who killed the crew! Did you kill the captain? Did you kill the cook? Did you threaten to kill Antonio? Did you torture Senor Montez?"

There was no need for any racial slurs; it's all in his tone. Cinque rose slowly, stared unflinchingly with a slight smile at the posturing Hollabird, and in counterpoint to Hollabird's tirade, he absorbed Hollabird's hate, building a strength of his own from the hate. Cinque did not know all the words Hollabird used he did know the tone, and the body language. Covey interpreted as fast as he could. There was a hush as the final questions were translated. Cinque looked at Hollabird, then at the judge. He let his blanket slide to the floor. In a rich full voice Cinque spoke Mende.

Like a foreign opera, his language may not have been understood by the audience, but the meaning was carried by the emotions of his face and voice. Cinque began slowly in Mende, unravelling the indignations and injustices that had bound them. Then, eloquently, holding his wrists and hands up as if shackled to show his scarred wrists, he raised his eyes glaring to heaven, he began to unfold his long story. As a branch flows to a creek, a creek to a stream, to the river, faster and faster to floodwaters, there built an emotion so strong that James Covey could not keep pace with the words. It was the pain in his voice and the dignity of his presence that demanded the attention of the room. They could no longer look at the interpreter, they were forced to Cinque. They did not need Covey's words to understand the pure emotions that were laid bare in front of them.

Cinque's face and body spoke for him. Then, almost as the court was won, as Cinque's voice flooded the room, he raised his hands to heaven and implores in English.

The court room gasped as he cried, "Give us free! Give us free!" Part demand, part plea, Cinque's words rang in the room's silence.

Then, realizing the reaction on the hushed court Hollabird shouted, "I object, take this man out of court, he will have an unfair influence on the decisions."

But it is too late. Every free man in the courtroom saw that what was his own right, this man Cinque had to fight for.

In that stark quiet Rodger Baldwin stood to complete his part of the defense. "I trust the court will free itself from all pressures, and act only in the interest of justice for these unfortunate people. For them, justice lies in being returned to Africa, to their families and homes, free to pursue their own way of life. As for me, I can do no better than repeat the words of Cinque, 'Give us free!'"

The judge banged his mallet and growled, unheard in the noise of the students and reporters rehashing the trial amongst themselves.

Adams pointed to a copy of the Declaration of Independence hanging on the courtroom wall, and said "I know no law, statute, or constitution, no code, no treaty, except that law...which [is] forever before the eyes of your Honors."

Delivered the opinion of the 7-1 majority the following decree:

"This Court having fully heard the parties appearing with their proofs, do find that the respondents, severally answering as aforesaid, are each of them natives of Africa, and were born free, and ever since have been, and still of right are free, and not slaves, as is in said several libels claims or representations alleged or surmised; that they were never domiciled in the Island of Cuba, or the dominions of the Queen of Spain, or subject to the laws thereof; that they were severally kidnapped in their native country, and were, in violation of their own rights, and of the laws of Spain, prohibiting the African slave trade, imported into the island of Cuba, about the 12th June, 1839, and were there unlawfully held and transferred to the said Ruiz and Montez, respectively; that said respondents were within fifteen days after their arrival at Havana, aforesaid, by said Ruiz and Montez, put on board said schooner Amistad to be transported to some port in said island of Cuba, and there unlawfully held as slaves; that the respondents or some of them, influenced by the desire of recovering their liberty, and of returning to their families and kindred in their native country, took possession of said schooner Amistad, killed the captain and cook, and severely wounded said Montez, while on her voyage from Havana, as aforesaid, and that the respondents arrived in possession of said schooner at Culloden Point near Montauck, and there anchored said schooner on the high seas, at the distance of half a mile from the shore of Long Island, and were there, while a part of the respondents were, as is alleged in their said answer, on shore in quest of water and other necessaries, and about to sail in said schooner for the coast of Africa, seized by said Lieutenant Gedney, and his officers and crew, and brought into the port of New London, in this district. And this Court doth further find, that it hath ever been the intention of the said Montez and Ruiz, since the said Africans were put on board the said schooner, to hold the said Africans as slaves; that at the time when the said Cinque and others, here making answer, were imported from Africa into the dominions of Spain, there was a law of Spain prohibiting such importations, declaring the persons so imported to be free; that said law was in force when the claimants took the possession of the said Africans and put them on board said schooner, and the same has ever since been in force."

Atkin finished his last sketch, was one of the last in the court room. The sun was low in the window and flared full on the eagle. Atkin closed his pad, looked around the nearly empty room, leaned next to the old reporter and asked, "What just happened?"

"Well, the majority said 'give him free.' Thompson, Taney, Story, Wayne, McLean Catron and McKinley with only one Dissent. Baldwin. Whoda guessed."

"John Quincy Adams, the astutest, archest enemy of southern slavery that ever existed."—*Henry Wise governor of Virginia*

It was precisely that rising characterization of John Quincy Adams that led his name to be reviled in the South and celebrated in the North and East. No wonder, then, that in 1841 abolitionist leaders requested Adams to defend before the Supreme Court the thirty-three remaining Africans involved in seizing the slave ship *Amistad*. A victory in this case would represent a symbolic victory for the civil rights of slaves and inhumanely dispersed Africans everywhere. Using a defense based on Baldwin's earlier defense Adams delivered a nine-hour address before the Supreme Court, a speech that would be hailed by Justice Joseph Story "for its power, for its bitter sarcasm, and for its dealing with topics far beyond the record and points of discussion." The captive defendants were freed, and hundreds of copies of Adam's speech were published throughout the North.

John Quincy Adams was quoted in the newspapers saying, "The trial on the Amistad, with Cinque as judge, was primitive. But, the emotions put forward in this trial were no less so. The dance and music of the Mende ritual were no more ritual than the formalities and posturing of this court. Here, the entire journal of the slaves was dramatized before the court. At the close of my 63,000 word summary the court's decision was favorable. Cinque and the thirty-five others were returned to Sierra Leone three years after their capture. This was not just a trial, but the beginning of a much larger battle. The moment you come to the Declaration of Independence, that every man has a right to life and liberty, an inalienable right—this case is decided, I ask nothing more on behalf of these unfortunate men, than this Declaration."

The trial was over. The courtroom filed out. The court was still. Rays of light glared through the old pressed glass of the courtroom window. The gold leafed eagle glowed like a beacon in sunlight against the stark white wall.

"Facts are stubborn things; and whatever
may be our wishes, our inclinations, or
the dictates of our passion, they cannot
alter the state of facts and evidence."

—*John Quincy Adams*

THE END

Well, that really wasn't the end.

November 25, 1841,The surviving Amistad Africans did make it back to Africa. Cinque returned with the rest. His family could not be found. His entire village had been burned and his family sold into slavery.

Many events led to the civil war, but the Amistad case was one event that filled newspapers north and south and hardened the passions, stirred fears, and created barriers between slavers and abolitionists that ended in Americas bloodiest war.

April 9, 1865 Northern victory established an indivisible nation, ended slavery and set the United States on a course that would eventually broaden democratic freedoms for all Americans.

Some called him crazy. Others called him
Old Man Eloquent. Most called him…

That Damned Adams

Much has been written about John Quecy Adams. He was, at 73, a shrewd, tough, ex-president, a lawyer, and a member of congress, then he tried and won a case before the Supreme Court that many say forced the Civil war. This novel is about the time, the place, and the people who reacted to that time, and why they did.

During a storm, sixty slaves broke free and took over the ship "Amistad". Three of the crew escaped, three others and the Captain were killed.

Their abduction in Africa, their revolt, the auction pens in Cuba, their ill-fated flight to freedom and capture off Rhode Island are woven into their trial—and behind the scenes political power plays in world politics.

Knowing how to sail the Amistad kept the two Cuban slave traders alive. The Africans spoke no Spanish. The cabin boy spoke some Mende , some Mandingo, and some Spanish. Cingue, the leader, had one driving passion: return to Africa. After many tries Cingue's orders were translated in broken Spanish. The Cubans couldn't believe it. The ship was too small for such a trip. They had no food, water. Cingue the hunter knew only how to follow the sun, the stars were a mystery to him. But he knew Africa was East. He would hear no other answer.

The Cuban's sailed for Africa by day, at night they came about for the coast of America. Battered by hurricanes, and short of food, week by week they zigzagged up the American coast. Finally, stopped by the US Navy off Long Island, they were arrested for Piracy. Newspapers north and south were aflame with wild accounts of the African pirates.

France, England, Spain, and America had signed an agreement twenty years prior not to trade in slaves anymore. But Spain looked the other way as its colony Cuba funneled hundreds of thousands of new slaves into southern America. President Van Buren, a pro slaver, wanted to give the "Amistad pirates" to Spain to hang. The slave-ocracy just wanted to hang Adams.

Fist fights broke out in congress. Reporters were stoned, their presses destroyed. There were riots from Boston to Baton Rouge. Adams was threatened with death or worse if he took the case. So he took the case ... and won. Their case enflamed the South and helped start a war.

DON'T QUIT

John Greenleaf Whittier

When things go wrong, as they sometimes will,
And the road you have to travel seems all uphill,
When the funds are low and the debts are high
And you want to smile, but you have to sigh,
When care is pressing you down a bit,
Rest if you must, but don't you quit.
Life is queer with its twists and turns,
As every one of us sometimes learns,
And many a failure turns about
When he might have won had he stuck it out.
Don't give up though the pace seems slow—
You may succeed with another blow.
Success is failure turned inside out—
The silver tint of the clouds of doubt,
And you never can tell how close you are,
It may be near when it seems so far;
So stick to the fight when you're hardest hit—
It's when things seem worst
that you must not quit.